I0649545

Pulse
Issue 2024-25
The Literary Magazine of Lamar University

Department of English and Modern Languages

LITERARY PRESS
LAMAR UNIVERSITY

Dedication

This edition of Pulse is dedicated to Dr. Sharon Joffe and Mr. John Rutherford, two gifted and inspirational writers.

Pulse Staff

Chief Student Editor
  Keely Viator
  Claudia Cooper

Typesetter
  Mikaela Bartlett

Poetry Editor
  Britton Larson
  Mae Bradley

Prose Editor
  Claudia Cooper
  Savanna Peveto-Kreatschman

Prose and Poetry Readers
  Erica Callahan
  Isabelle Deese
  Mikaela Bartlett
  Christine Osborne
  Grace Nicholson
  Grace Harmon
  Jazmin Gonzalez

Cover Art: "Savior" by Nyah Greene

Faculty Advisor
  Katherine Hoerth
  Theresa Ener

Department Chair
  Sara Hillin

Faculty Judges
  Casey Ford
  Adam Nemmers
  Jim Sanderson
  Gretchen Johnson

Publication
  Lamar University Press

Awards

Poetry — "The Architect" by Mae Bradley

Poetry-in-Translation — "AMOR" by Mae Bradley, translated from Antonio Gamoneda

Short Fiction — "Cowboys" by Danny Young

Creative Nonfiction — "The Execution of Lady Jane Grey" by Grace Harmon

Scholarly Essay — "The Harlot Wears Scarlet: Symbolism in Chaucer's "The Canterbury Tale"" by Savanna Peveto-Kreatschman

Art — "Savior" by Nyah Greene

Contents

Poetry

Poetry in Translation

Short Fiction

Creative Non-Fiction

Scholarly Essays

Art

Alumni Spotlight

Farm
Ann Manes

What a good, good life
of quilts
jellies
canned beans we grew ourselves
and dillpickling the dewfresh cucumbers

Lie in bed
in the soft sweet night
and hear a horse,
a whippoorwill,
an owl.
Cattle low
Geese call —

In the morning they hiss
when I pick up a gosling
that feels like a dusty ball of nothing.

Take a hookless line to the pond
and feed Wheaties to the perch.
Go to another pond —
the stagnant pond —
and feel the slow creeping peace.

Back to the cool wellhouse
where the dog and cat nap.
Wash the clothes
bleach them in the sun
and sit in solitude
on Swedish Grandpa's butcher block.

Especially Seahorse Jim
Ann Manes

I put the quilt — the old one from the porch —
On the grass — the grass I've needed to mow for a while now —
To watch the meteor shower as promised
A plane ambled by
Two UFOs — the space station maybe
Felt thankful for the soft grass
   the night sky
   the oak tree
   the smell of the gardenias
   the balmy night air
Thought about the loved ones who have passed
   — friends, not lovers —
   — mainly Sea Horse Jim —
   but others, too — too late
   to make sure they knew
   I really loved them
   — especially Sea Horse Jim —
After the mosquitos found me
   and invited their cousins
I shook out the quilt and went in
Not minding anymore about the meteors

Ann Manes has been writing poetry since fifth grade. Years later, she spent a year acting with a traveling theater company, the Alpha Omega Players. She raised four children with then-husband David Hooker. Manes served in the U.S. Coast Guard Reserve for eight years, on active duty during the Operation Desert Storm/Shield. She went to law school at the University of Houston and spent fifteen years as a Jefferson County assistant district attorney. During that time, Manes returned to Lamar University to earn her M. A. in English.

Poetry

Interjection
Davonna Martin

I don't know what to do
with this agony welded deep into my chest.
I taped euphoria above it, but the tape isn't as strong.
it's only momentarily, but I constantly tape it
down in hopes that it stays.

The mind is filled with invalidated thoughts
and contradictions.
and nothing ever lasts long, nor does it improve.
I walked a long way, turned around, and walked back.

an angry little girl who can never get her emotions under control.
an angry adult who can never make sense of them.
You know what you want, and you know what you need to do.
yet, you allow yourself to reminisce in your
dejection and it is no one's fault but yours

you miss it and you allow yourself to relive in that familiarity
and that is why you will never get better.
You rely on nothing but distractions and
other people to give you that sense of
felicity.

If nothing happened, was it even real?
if no one knows the full length, does it even matter?
Was it ever something if you have nothing to show for it?

You envy those who made the decision to let it go and let it be.
you resent yourself because you can never
make that decision without the feelings of
others on your mind.

You're ending this with anger for the reason
no one sees how much you try.
this is your home now. you've built it
now live in it.

All Good Things
Vanessa Davis

Triangles, clovers, the holy trinity
Things that work in *unity*
Pyramids, musketeers, time of day
Things that last and things that *stay*
Olympic medals, wisemen, dimensions
None of these have *exemptions*,
All good things come in three,
So why didn't we?

Angel
Mikaela Bartlett

Tell me I'm wrong
Tell me
Whisper it into my ear, make your warm breath brush past my
defenses
The breath you took from me.
I can't count how many times I should've left on twenty hands
Thirty hands
However many hands you have, however many faces,
however many lies
You were so beautiful in your heavenly disguise
The morning sun will shine
The nighttime moon will rise
But you will always be a devil in disguise
You are a broken one
An aching, beating string of lies yet to come undone
And I can still feel your breath on me
Your warm breath, brushing past my defenses
The breath you took from me.
I can't take my eyes off your broken, tattered, torn and shattered
wings
Because you are just an angel fallen down
And I just thought to catch you.

Home Sick
Mikaela Bartlett

The reds of West Texas
and the swamps of the South and Louisiana border
curling around my wrist like a rattler
keeping me tethered to the rich land I know

The heat of the dry summer's air
the suffocating and draining
the lone starry burden flaming
leftover from days of the crow

And who could forget the bluebonnet fields?
rich purples and blues so bright, so striking
southern hospitality so humble, so inviting
that lone star in the sky turned orange and indigo

The smokey flavors of good ol' Texas foods
hand-cut meats, plucked straight from the fields
always a drink to accompany a meal
lending a hand to your neighbor fellow

From the brights and sights of Houston
to the salty taste of the Gulf, the layers of the desert
traveling to the deepest corner of the heart
from below the sea to the highest plateau

Starting at the beginning, and on to the next
the landscape shifts with the people, the places
a land blessed in God's good graces
the beautiful star so lone

Eight Months
Mikaela Bartlett

I ran into an old friend last week,
at the coffee shop, where everyone runs into old friends
we hugged, said the other looked so good
she promised to text me when she's back in town
I know she won't.
we'll move on,
run into each other again in eight months or so
she will be engaged; I will be engaged
she will own a house; I will own a house
her mother has died; my grandfather has died
she adopted two cats; I've sworn off litter boxes
she looks like me
I look like her
she won't have texted
it's fine
we've moved on.
we'll run into each other again in eight months or so.

Mosaic of Misjudgements
Gaberielle LaRocca

I'm misunderstood
It's thought that I'm up to no good
Just want to be in my adulthood
Don't wanna be reminded of my childhood
Supposed to make a nice livelihood
My likelihood of being amazing isn't so good
And I would rather deal with the truths than being fake and acting
like it's all good.
How could one?
How should one?
How would one?
Just gonna be gone for good
Just a piece of driftwood

Confessions of a Broken Porcelain Doll
Maci Simmons

I lay here,
gazing at my shattered pieces,
my heart tied
to a life-support machine
gasping hushed, meek breaths
thoughts circle 'round me
ghosts of a grim past.

I wonder endlessly,
the word FRAGILE
in bold, beaming ink
handled so carelessly,
tossed, turned, thrown, tortured,
expectations clear
yet shocked by the outcome.

I smile vigorously,
my soul cries
silent agony
beauty now in shambles,
enriched appearance
forever tainted
poor, inexperienced hands.

Content
Rylee Wenzel

Sitting in silence.
The kind that is like a Sunday morning.
Slow and soft and never asking for more.

The crackle of bacon in the pan.
The constant drip of coffee.
Silently moving as we prepare
For our day.

Love that is quiet.
Quiet like waves crashing in the middle of the night.
Simple, yet great and powerful all at once.

Loving you is like taking a breath.

Be Heard
Kowen Ducote

I take my boots off the floor
And skate my way to the podium
I stand upon two legs
And an ear muffled by my people

I stand at this podium with a purpose
But subconsciously I was nervous
That when I spoke the wires
And cords of the mic would choke
Wrap around my throat

As I drop to the floor
I can feel the oxygen leaving my body
The over-intoxication from the night before
Was a decision that was lousy

So I stand at this podium slurring my words
Making my people heard
If I represent 'em bad
Then am I the good & the ugly
'Cause it seems the more I stumble & fall
The louder the chants get
The tighter the mic sits
Upon my neck ready to
Constrict & end this nightshift

In my final breaths I ask you today
Are you happy with yourself?
Finding the power within the evil,
Are you proud of your wealth?
I might never get the got
The cars, the fame, the shame that you got
But what I stand for is a fight you ain't shot
A fire that burns bright
A liar that sounds nice
But when he deceives he moves in asynchronous rhythms
Venomous spit to the ears, for him it's an algorithm
Systemic, cynical, hell it's even fatherly
When you sever that artery
Blood spews out the limbs of harmony

Into the pools of sisters and brothers
We do admire
Fighting an everlasting battle
We don't desire
But we keep doing and it's sanctioned by greed
A cyclical cycle of barely meeting our needs
If they can hear us from way up above
Your shallow desires will never compare to the love

They say it's the mark of the beast
I say it's the mark of the deed
Of those who got more influence, power, & fame than me
So if I got one last thing to say
Before the mic strikes and if I
End up on the news today
If I have two final words, to set us free
Confined, Shackled down, Bottled up—
Be Heard.

Inspired by J.Cole's "Be Free"
In honor of the Blackout Strikes and the push for Palestine's liberation

Manner of Men
Kensi MacCammond Williams

A found poem taken from an excerpt of Dracula by Bram Stoker:

This time, there is no doubt in question—
I shall fear to sleep in any place where he is not.
My rest is thus freer,
My dreams there shall remain.

When he left me, I came out
towards the vast expanse inaccessible to me,
the narrow darkness of prison I seemed to want;
I feel this existence destroying my nerve.

My own shadow full of horrible imaginings—
God knows my terrible fear.
This accursed place bathed in shadows,
velvety blackness in every breath.

My eye caught what I imagined—
that of the Count: tall and deep,
stone-mullioned, complete;
I drew back carefully.

I knew the man by the movement of his mistake:
hands studying, interested and amused;
how small a matter will interest and amuse a man
when he is prisoner.

My very feelings changed when I saw
that dreadful abyss spreading out around him,
great wings of moonlight, shadow, delusion.
I grasp every projection—inequality, a wall.

What manner of man is this—
overpowering me?
I am in awful fear there is no escape,
For I am encompassed about with that I dare think of.

Her Desire's Will
Kensi MacCammond Williams

A found poem taken from an excerpt of Blood Countess by Lana Popović:

I don't believe this is wrong—
Her teeth, my skin, I gasp;
"Who else could know *your* desire
better than I?"

She draws me around her—
Eyes lustrous, palms to cheeks;
for who could know better
than another woman?

"No one," I whisper—
Move to unlace my desire, obliterate modesty;
restraint never fathomed such
delicious, honeyed madness.

"Then abandon shame and come,"
commands the raven-haired siren offering me *her*.

Even Now
Erica Callahan

I-10 Eastbound, towards the Sabine
Going 65, feeling 90
in the dark
Things move much faster
Just me and the semi-truck
And the cop with ghost lettering waiting
For our slip-up
And the man swerving between the lanes that we don't
Get too close to
Lest we end up broken like him
Afraid of the circumstances and
yourself
What choices lead us here

Stained Glass
Teri Wolfe

In your hands
I am made whole

from sand into glass.

I am of many colors,
tiny grits, and fragments—

and you,
you are light. You are warmth.

Hand in hand, we create
a cascade of reflections,
our own rainbow sun.

We are a sacrilegious prism.
A church's own windows

will never seem as holy.

Sisterhood Sold Separately
Moya Rose

Sister? Don't call me sister—
your sisterhood? I can't afford it.
The price is steep, the terms unfair,
your allyship stops when you have to care.

You march with me, sign in hand,
but only if the photos land.
Equality's fine, as long as it's clear
that you stay center, and I'm nowhere near.

You champion the fight, bold and bright,
but your solidarity fades at night.
When power's at stake, or gains might stall,
you disappear, if you show up at all.

You smile wide, say all the right things,
but behind my back, the knife still stings.
You lift me up, then watch me fall,
climbing higher on us all.

You want my voice, but not too loud,
my culture—only when it's allowed.
My pain? A prop, my rage? A phase,
your sympathy comes in fleeting waves.

So no, don't call me sister here.
Your "unity" is insincere.
Your justice? A self-serving sport—
your sisterhood, I can't afford.

Following is a collection of formal poems written by Jiyoon Jeon with the themes of winter, healing, resilience, and hope.

Contents

#1. Meaning of Winter

Winter is cold and gray, a bleak domain,
Where life seems lost beneath the heavy sky,
The frozen winds remind us of our pain,
And darkness whispers, making spirits cry.

Yet in this quiet, still and stark retreat,
The earth prepares for life to bloom again;
A time for rest, for healing, soft and sweet,
Where hope lies dormant, free from toil or strain.

For every frost will melt beneath the sun,
And every night will fade to morning's light;
The cycle spins, and though the winter's done,
New strength is born from silence and the night.

So in the cold, there lies a hidden grace—
A time for rest to heal and soul embrace.

#2. Winter-Melting Memory

In winter's chill, we built our snowman tall,
With snowflakes swirling in the frosty air,
Then sipped our cocoa, feeling warm and small.

The world outside was quiet, soft, and all
A canvas white, with dreams so pure and fair,
In winter's chill, we built our snowman tall.

The cold on our cheeks, a frigid, bright call,
But inside, the warmth was ours to share,
Then sipped our cocoa, feeling warm and small.

With laughter echoing, we'd sometimes fall,
Into the snow, without a single care,
In winter's chill, we built our snowman tall.

As steam rose from mugs, it seemed to install
A sense of peace, beyond the world we'd dare,
Then sipped our cocoa, feeling warm and small.

Now years have passed, but I still can recall
The joy of those days, so bright and rare,
In winter's chill, we built our snowman tall,
Then sipped our cocoa, feeling warm and small.

#3. Reunification

Across distant seas,
Their laughter fades with the breeze,
Home is far from me.

155 miles between,
Silent winds carry my heart,
Home calls from afar.

Silent nights I wait,
Unseen shadows fill my mind,
Is their breath still warm?

Through the storm we stand,
Hope's light guides us through the dark,
We will meet again.

By God's mercy and grace,
In heaven's warm light, souls embraced,
We will meet again.

#4. Snowflake, Beauty of Ephemeralness

A snowflake falls soft from the sky,
So delicate, drifting nearby.
It sparkles, then fades,
In the cold winter shades,
A moment, then gone as it flies.

#5. Kindness

For every kind word given with care,
I'm filled with gratitude deep and true.
In this world, such kindness is rare,
For every kind word given with care.
It lifts my heart, removes despair,
A gift so precious, always anew.
For every kind word given with care,
I'm filled with gratitude deep and true.

#6. Kindness 2

In words, we could find a kinder way,
Yet violence builds walls we cannot see.
Why must we fight, when we could choose to say,
In words, we could find a kinder way?
The hate we sow will only lead astray,
While peace is found where hearts and minds agree.
In words, we could find a kinder way,
Yet violence builds walls we cannot see.

#7. Winter Color

The winter's breath is pure and cold,
A quiet white that fills the sky,
Yet in its depths, new hues unfold,
From softest pink to amber high.
A snowy veil with colors bold,
It paints the dawn, the dusk, the sigh.
The purity of winter's grace,
In every flake, a world embraced,
Where white can hold each shade and trace,
And all the colors find their place.

#8. Winter Embraces Night

In winter's grasp, the darkness holds the night,
A quiet hush that swallows all the sound.
The coffee warms my hands, a comforting grace,
While frost outside coats earth with icy ground.
But deep within, I long for spring's light,
A time when life returns with warmth and embrace.

The winter nights seem endless, void of light,
With shadows stretching far through endless night.
I sip my coffee, hoping for a grace
Of spring to stir the quiet in the ground.
But still, I wait, the cold a harsh embrace,
My thoughts alight on days when warmth will sound.

Each sip of tea, a hope with a cheerful sound
Away the cold, to find a spark of light.
For winter's cruel, though spring will soon embrace
The chill with sunshine, melting frozen night.
I dream of blossoms pushing through the ground,
Of green and life returning, full of grace.

And yet, for now, I find no gentle grace,
Just bitter winds that through the branches embrace
The warmth of spring, to freeze it in the ground.
My coffee, dark, a shield against the night,
A fleeting moment's warmth, a fleeting light,
But still, I wait for spring to take its sound.

For in the winter's dark, I long for embrace
Where flowers bloom and spring returns with grace.
I cling to hope, to warmth, to chase, to light
The shadows that the cold and night sound.
Yet coffee fills my cup, and tea fills night,
Both soothing me as cold bites into ground.

As cold persists, my dreams of spring ground,
And though the night holds tight, I trust its sound.
For even winter's dark will fade with light,
And soon, the ground will pulse with life and grace.

Until then, I sip my tea, my coffee, my night
The warmth within, while waiting for the embrace.

Beneath the stars, the world feels still at night,
In quiet moments, I am filled with grace,
And dawn arrives, breaking through with soft light.

#9. O Winter, Thy Melty Beauty

O Winter, thou art sovereign of the cold,
With frosted breath that paints the world so white,
Thy beauty, though in silence harsh and bold,
Reveals the depth of Nature's quiet might.
Thy crystal winds do sweep the barren land,
Yet in thy grasp, there blooms a secret grace,
For all the seeds within thy frozen hand
Shall rise again in Spring's renewing pace.
Thy snow, like gentle whispers, blankets deep,
A silent hymn that calms the restless earth.
Within thy stillness, life begins to sleep,
Yet stirs below, awaiting Spring's rebirth.
The pines stand firm beneath thy frosty veil,
Their branches bearing burdens soft and true,
While all the world, beneath thy touch, grows pale,
Yet finds in thee a path for life anew.
Thy nights are long, thy days are short and clear,
A time for rest, a moment's sweet reprieve.
Yet in the dark, the stars do reappear,
And whisper of the promise we believe.
For in thy grasp, O Winter, lies the key
To all that follows, from the leaf to bloom.
A cycle, bound in timeless harmony,
Where life and death find meaning in thy womb.
So let us praise thee, Winter, bold and wise,
For though thy chill may bite, and winds may roar,
Thy reign prepares the soil where life shall rise,
And Spring, with warmth, will open Nature's door.
In thee, O Winter, we find peace and trust,
For thou art but the herald of the dawn,
A promise wrapped in snow, serene and just,
That life, through cycles, always will be drawn.

#10. The Eternal Winter

I. The Winter's First Chill

In days long past, when Korea stood tall,
A land of beauty, rich in art and lore,
The winds of fate did blow with bitter call,
And shadows darkened hearts and closed the door.
Yet in the cold, where many would despair,
The spirit of the land would still endure,
For through the frost, the Korean heart did flare,
With strength unbroken, firm and ever pure.
The first of winters came with chilling breath,
A time of hardship, loss, and stolen land,
Yet Koreans stood against the march of death,
Their courage stronger than a mighty band.
When foreign hands would grasp and steal their pride,
The people's fire could not be quenched or bent,
For in the winter's cold, they did not hide—
Their souls burned bright with hope, and firm intent.

II. The Longest Night

The winter grew, its nights so deep and long,
The winds that howled could freeze a heart of stone,
Yet still the people's voices, soft but strong,
Would echo through the dark, a steady tone.
Though kingdoms fell and kingdoms rose in haste,
Korea's heart refused to fall or break,
For even in the coldest, harshest waste,
The warmth of hope, like fire, would never quake.
Through nights of sorrow, silence, and despair,
When rulers came and sought to crush the soul,
The people held, though none could see them there,
Their hearts as steadfast as the mountain's roll.
They faced the frost with steady, silent eyes,
And in their hearts, the winter would not stay.
For though the darkest hour filled the skies,
The dawn would come and cast the dark away.

III. Beneath the Snow, the Roots Still Grow

Beneath the snow, the seeds began to sleep,
A quiet world where silence ruled the ground,
Yet in the stillness, life began to creep,

With roots that reached, though buried deep, unbound.
For winter's grip, though harsh, could not erase
The spirit of a people born to rise.
In every wound, in every cold embrace,
A seed of strength was planted to the skies.
The frost may freeze the earth, yet hearts remain
Alive with stories passed through winds and snow,
A people's will, like roots beneath the plain,
Would stretch and fight, though none could see it grow.
And though the night was long, the time would come
When from the frozen earth, the light would break.
For winter's cold can only numb, not numb
The hearts of those who in the darkness wake.

IV. The Winter's End

And though the storms would rage and nights would weep,
And many souls would fall beneath the tide,
The Korean heart, unbroken, would not sleep,
For in the cold, they held the flame inside.
And through the ice, the world would find its way,
A dawn, though distant, promised to arrive,
For every winter has its final day,
And in the end, the soul shall still survive.
So as the days grow dark, and frost returns,
Remember how the Korean spirit stands,
For though the cold may bite, the fire burns,
And in the heart, the warmth will still command.
No winter's chill, no night's unyielding reign,
Can ever quell the flame that rises bright—
For after every storm, the sun will reign,
And lead us through the darkest, coldest night.

V. The Eternal Flame

Now in this winter, harsh and full of fear,
When storms of change and loss seem to divide,
Look to the past, to those who once were here,
Who faced the night with courage, undenied.
For in their struggle, strength and hope were sown,
A seed that grows beyond the frost and flame,
A story told, from mountain's peak to stone,
Of how the Korean heart can never tame.
Through every winter's cold and endless night,

The flame will burn, and through the darkest skies,
We find our strength, our courage, and our light,
In every tear, a new dawn slowly rises.
So when the winds of winter blow again,
And cold surrounds, remember this refrain:
No matter how the storms may strike and bend,
The heart of Korea shall endure the pain.

Hold On
Nyah Greene

Her petals have fallen but she still holds on
She watches everyone grow their petals back
Confused on why hers haven't formed
Day by day passes by watching others grow
"Why am I still without my petals, she begins,
The feeling of being bare, exposed is uncomfortable
She lost her petals before me but hers grew back instantly"
She began to wilt

Her form has become unrecognizable but she still holds on
Hoping her petals will return one day
She decided to close her eyes, darkness consumed her
Wrapped up in herself, only focusing on her
A peak of light shown through an opening
Warmth then consumed her, feeling revived
Stretching out amongst the sun with petals rippling around her
Her petals have grown majestically, yet she still holds on

I am made for so much more than this:
an homage to what I can still be
Teri Wolfe

Somehow, I've let paper betray me.
I was a friend, an ally.
with my pencil,
we charged into battle together
like sword and shield.
Oh, how we have fallen since then.
Now my old comrade sits in stacks,
begging, desperate to be sorted.
Was the war over?

Maybe it's the cheap pens talking,
but every time I try again
the ink runs dry.
A fight I keep losing,
nothing left but empty dialogue
and dial-tone messages.
Lit up behind dual monitors,
I stage a silent protest in my head:

I know I shine brighter than
a bunch of pixelated data,
sorted in their own formations
of columns and rows.
With my stapled flag at half-mast—
not in surrender,
but in mourning of all the time
and ideas lost to monotonous labor—
I know this is not an impasse.

I must rebuild again.
I will keep sketching,
whether on sticky notes
with branded corporate logos on top,
or on college-ruled, yellow-paged notepads.
My swivel chair will be my chariot,
a squeaky throne of secret defiance,
and I will make this office
regret me.

Santos Rodriguez: A Brother, Son, and Human
Jarely Rebollar

Killed

Rock-throwing Mexican-Americans,
windows smashed,
disrupting traffic,
and Police motorcycles attacked,

Half a dozen policemen injured,
chasing demonstrators from City Hall.
Milling bands prowled,
Dallas march turns violent.

A twelve-year-old boy
killed

The Brown Berets obtained a permit,
to march and protest the fatal shooting.
Twelve hundred gathered at City Hall,
emotions damaged.

Patrolman, murder indicted,
remained in jail, bond set at fifty thousand.
Councilman attempted to calm the crowd,
but a woman took over the microphone.

Santos Rodriguez
a twelve-year-old boy
killed

What Circles the Lighthouse
Keely Viator

For Bolivar Point Lighthouse

Mortared with brick, mothered with cast iron,
the lighthouse calls for all children—
the well-established freighter
with the wrinkle of rust beneath its eyes,
or the darling, runted dinghy
and its pitter patter motor.

In sunny skies, it sits peaceful
by the shoreline, tallying
seagulls that perch on its rails.
The wayward birds remain welcome
visitors so long as they leave a loose feather
before flying far from home.

In hurricanes, it holds solid,
walls sloping into a slick dropped cradle.
The windowsill sounds a hushing plea
where the rain thunders against it,
a brewing child that wears
none of the ears to hear it out.

Steadfast, it hollows into a shelter,
introducing itself as a gracious guardian
that lifts unexpected guests to safety.
It plays peekaboo, beacon kissing the storm's forehead,
no matter how loud the frantic wave tantrums
and pounds its saltwater fists against the lighthouse's side.

Croaker's Dilemma
Keely Viator

These frogs are both a world swallowing
and a creature daring to be swallowed by the world.

Those eighteen toes of theirs make the bold claim
they could jump a chasm without a sweat, effortless.

Their ideal night is green in the pond's muddy swell,
each of their jade-stone forms nestled among chirring food,

a dragon hiding in its hoard. Unguarded insects mount
the backs of these aggregate bodies given life, reckless tamers.

Then that feral jade façade splits, their mouths open, tongues
unfurl to swipe a swarm inward unbeknownst to their rider.

Wingless, they must be prepared to fall far each time they kick off,
their hind legs working up the nerve to make the next leap,

croaking their well wishes to the wayward sky as they glide.
They lean both on hope the water deep will be kind

and that their own bodies will latch when they hit surface,
clinging onto the first structure that will forgive their trespass.

But the Heart is Missing
Keely Viator

The house builds up lungs to breathe in smoke,
its siding warping like infected skin
as it plants itself, begging to be a home.
Let me in, let me in,
into your dust and particle,
your very pore.

A home is a sacred thing,
where ribs are stored in the kitchen fridge,
tongues kept in the bathroom sink,
and fingers kept on closet hangers.
The fact you allow guests in at all
is the mystery of what it means to be human,
to peer close into another's business.

To feel at home, it makes sense a house
should come to possess you as you possess it,
infested with your dead hairs and flaking skin,
a stationary effigy resembling clothes too substantial
to fit well on human bodies. Natural anxiety of this inability
to grow in leads you to share your architectural burden,
a family plot, a companion grave. Lie down in your beds

and look up to the dimpled ceiling.
Through swollen eyes, the stucco will peer back.

Let Sleeping Shelves Lie
Keely Viator

There's something sharp about several books stacked on a table,
a guard dog built from ink and glue, curled up in wait.
As I pass, I imagine it turning suddenly, teeth bared and snapping.
At least then there would be warning to peeking over books
I would make too poor of a foster to bring home.

Instead, I watch them press forward against the library table,
hard surface meeting soft volume as their head leaks
dream upon dream into a room built around stories, a drool
I need to be careful not to slip in, or I will be stuck to that dusty carpet
until the custodian comes to wipe both of us up.

A waking book poses another threat, the thudding bark
of a cover slamming open and closed as a clamor of words rise,
centering themselves in a helpless readers head, touching their heart and
leaving them with some newer than expected from such sepia pages. In
my mind, the books at once stand on end, waiting to be called to sic.

What a horrifying thought,
the unread taking such swift and sudden revenge on a lazy reader.
But I still think a napping dog is hard to look away from
when its snoozing is so charming that it draws the eye, even in stillness,
and an alert dog draws me close, transforming me with its loyal earnesty.

Windowsill Thoughts
Shelby Eason

Cacti have spines because
They have soft centers.
Venus Flytraps bite because
Their soil is too barren.

My center is soft.
I stab.
My soul is barren.
I bite.

Orchids bloom when
They are well taken care of.
I want to have their flowers
To show that I am kind.
Trees grow tall and sturdy,
Their branches stretch into places they do not know.
I want to have their branches
So people can sit next to me and enjoy my shade
And rest their backs on my sturdy trunk
And not worry if I will fall when they lean on me.

I want to rip off my spines,
Allow someone the injury of
Burrowing into my soft center.
I want to rip out my teeth,
Give someone the opportunity to
Pollinate my lonely soul without
Fearing my jaws.

I want flowers.
I want branches.
I want shade.
I want strength.

I have spines.
I have teeth.
My center is soft.
I stab.

My soul is barren.
I bite.

I grow.

House for Sale
Chloe Lopez

A house on 32 Orleans Road,
By the Rising Sun cafe,
Sat for sale like a toad,
On a mushroom stool.

The realtor tried everything,
Open houses, free cookies,
Even classes on table setting,
But to no avail.

The house was quite lovely, yet
"Buyer beware" stood painted on a sign opposite the house,
The neighbors all afraid of the home, even the pets,
Urging prospective buyers to seek elsewhere.

One unlucky couple, down on their luck,
Inquired the asking price, and the realtor,
Wanting to make a quick buck,
Sold it on the spot for a McChicken and two dollars.

His wife, a known HGTV fanatic, stepped right in on closing day,
A smile on her face and tool belt in tow,
Looked high and low for ideas to flip the house every which way,
So the couple, addicted to get rich schemes, could buy low, sell high.

The couple painted a fresh coat of paint outside and in,
Removed the creepy kitten wallpaper and replaced it with millennial
grey,
Sanded the blood stained wood floors to place tile in
An underwhelming grey.

That first night the couple slept in their new bed,
The house groaned with age as it woke to its face lift,
The house, now completely devoid of any green, blue, or red,
Enacted revenge on its occupants.

Bookcases slammed on the floor,
Dishes broke mid air,
And open was every door,
The abode left no corner untouched.

The couple awoke with anxiety pangs,
The husband's heart gave out at the sight,
Of his favorite wall sconces no longer hang-
Ing.

The wife replaced the books, swept the glass,
Pushed off the thought of an angry spirit,
But ran to the balcony and threw herself onto the overpass,
When she saw the late governess ripping her West Elm throw pillows.

Late the next morning, the realtor stepped up,
Feet kicking spirit broken televisions and plywood tables,
Hands wiping at shredded wallpaper, overturned cups,
Eyes rolling at the dramatic response to the occupants.

Didn't they read the contract?
"Buyer beware, this house must remain in its original condition,
Lest you renovate it to high hell and back,
The old owners will come to right your wrongs."

A house on 32 Orleans Road croaks,
By the Rising Sun Cafe,
Sat for sale with two new folks,
Angry at the influencer who just set down a box of Greige abstract
paintings.

Father
Gabriela Valiente

I am envious of my father,
For he is able to leave and become a better person
While I pick up the pieces he left in his wake.
No, I do not hold that against him.
I am an adult and understand this had to happen.
He is not a bad person.
I love him very much.
But, at the end of the day,
I am reminded without fail
That he is a man
And will always act as one.

Bare
Cheyenne Lunsford

I could dream up a paint brush
to paint the leaves' hue
vibrant oranges, reds and golds too.

I could ask the wind to rush
and blow the leaves around
into an umber blanket for the cold ground,

but your brown boughs I'll never change,
for it could never dream to compare
to such an icy ancient beauty bare.

As branches with icy dustings hang
Mottled with brown and green.
It's vast, it's wild, serene.

So here I will linger, I will stay.
I will get lost in your sounds,
along with the critters nesting in your grounds.

It is home to them, and in a way,
the bitter bite of frosts boastful breeze,
warms my heart and sets my soul free.

A Modern Prayer
Mae Bradley

Once, my dentist told me she was tired of pulling teeth.
I thought that she had chosen the wrong career.

But now I'm grown up
And I pull teeth every day.
Nothing ever seems to go my way.

It's so messed up,
Sometimes I think
Everyone on this planet really stinks.

I'm doing my best
But no matter what I do,
The words that I say never get through.

I want to reason with you,
But you say I'm "too intense".
I'm starting to think that you're just dense.

I'm begging now,
I'm on my hands and knees
Please try to use your brain for once.

PLEASE.

The Good Fight
Mae Bradley

Love tastes like a mouthful of pennies.
A kiss is still a punch in the teeth.
To love another is to be on the winning side of a war.
There will still be blood.

Love is to fight, tooth and nail, for something bigger.
Love is to lose with purpose.
Compromise is the best-case scenario.
To love is to be shot
By a bullet that stops the consequent bleeding.

Love is a slow and painful death.
It is a hand held in the trenches.

The Architect
Mae Bradley

That which lies before me:
A gossamer bundle.
The finest black hairs that curl
In a spiral staircase,
Only to bridge the gap
Between your crown and eyes
And conceal the sweetest part of you.
Behind a screen of rungs,
Sideways as they might be,
I would climb up Jacob's ladder
Across the warm skin
That wraps your skull like paper on a gift.
A lifetime of learning
To a divine end in glorious understanding.
Though the world once made sense,
Without a god
Who turned the known into mystery,
Your company is evangelism
And I want to believe.

Fuzzbucket
Claudia Cooper

In the land of inbetween
there was a cat turd in my windowsill
Fuzzbucket's litterbox
overflowed with twice than average
a crapper
a scrapper
a wild thing we tamed by force-
tough love-
Declawed and Docile?
Will she still chitter and chatter away to me?
Even though kittens will never come
Even though Fuzzbucket is my baby forever
I'm scared I've done something
wrong again to my beloved
pet cat.
Is that why the land of inbetween
was watched over by a slit in the sky-
omniscient cat eye deciding it
was time for inevitable doom.
A Giant, Extraterrestrial, Black Cat Paw
swiping us from existence.

The Feline Nature of Poetry
Claudia Cooper

Poetry sunbathes on my windowsill
or naps in the dining chair in the corner.
Her perfect image strikes me as I pass,
but I dare not disturb her peace.
When she is ready, my bedroom door
bursts open, pat-pat-pat, Poetry's
soft rhythmic paws tap against wood.
Meow! Poetry demands my attention.
I can go ignored, but Poetry cannot.
Meow! Poetry is not satisfied
until I stroke her, feed her, and let her out.
Meow! Poetry calls on her way out as thanks.

If I go to Poetry before she is ready,
I am met with indifference.
Hooded eyes and the lazy turn of her head,
a few soft purrs as compensation
for her lackluster reception.
Even with all my coaxing,
Poetry only goes back to sleep
or worse, bites, when she tires of me.
I can only retreat in the hopes
her still image – of softness and
etherealness, a godly being –
is enough to satisfy.

Old Clothes
Britton Larson

You reap what you sow
And so would it seem
The seams of my clothes
Are close to tearing

I have these old jeans
These genes I've outgrown
I groan at the hems
The him I used to know

Like wine
Crystal Figueroa

How beautiful aging can be

Growing

Wiser

More beautiful

Your precious expressions planting its mark on your skin

Birthdays celebrating your anniversary with the world that would never be the same without you

Nothing to be ashamed, embrace the age

Every gray, wrinkle, and body change

I am grateful for how far our bodies and souls have come

You me and the moon
Crystal Figueroa

You are as precious and beautiful as the moon

Loved in every phase

Every crater embracing your flaws

The moon would not be as beautiful without its craters

Your craters simply make me love you more

Poetry in Translation

AMOR
Antonio Gamoneda

Mi manera de amarte es sencilla:
te aprieto a mí
como si hubiera un poco de justicia en mi corazón
y yo te la pudiese dar con el cuerpo.
Cuando revuelvo tus cabellos
algo hermoso se torna entre mis manos.
Y casi no sé más. Yo sólo aspiro
a estar contigo en paz y a estar en paz
con un deber desconocido
que a veces pesa también en mi corazón.

LOVE

My manner of loving you is simple:
I fix you to myself
like there's a little justice in my heart
and I could give it to you with my own body.

Whenever I ruffle your hair
something beautiful forms between my hands.

And I almost don't know anymore. I only aspire
to be with you in peace and to be at peace
with an unknown duty
that sometimes also weighs on my heart.

Translator's note
Mae Bradley

I undertook the task of translating a poem with the original purpose of bringing previously unnoticed material to the eyes of my peers in a way that would be digestible for them. Antonio Gamoneda is a poet I stumbled across in a search for Spanish language works that went unrecognized by English poetry translation. I became fascinated by Gamoneda's perspective of life and how those we care for give us purpose. He has written various works that exemplify the human experience of rebellion and autonomy. Gamoneda suspects that love is the heart of these, as it is a beautiful recognition of our own mortality and free will and he believes that life is made worthwhile by the strength love grants us. In "AMOR", he illustrates a picture of pure love, untainted by specifics of romance or relationship. The simplicity of the content in this poem allows readers to form individual connections between the work and their own lives regardless of the nature of their connections with loved ones.

This particular poem stole my heart with its universality, serving as a reminder of the value of human company of all sorts. I believe that as individuals, our lives are enriched by those who we interact with and we share the same potential to affect theirs in turn. Just as I had hoped to touch my peers with a newly accessible poem, I was touched by it as well. My translation pales in comparison to the original work, unable to perfectly replicate the precise language and distinct raw emotion produced by Gamoneda. My hope is to serve as an open door which will allow the reader to experience the original work with a sense of understanding and connection to the author. In this way, a great poetic mind can become yet another person who affects and enriches the lives of English-speaking scholars, a testament to the very subject of the poem I have translated.

Short Fiction

Silence
Vanessa Davis

"Bye Mom!" Jimmy yells as he skips through the old kitchen, aiming towards the kitchen's screen door.

"Okay, have fun dear, and remember to get back before dark! It's too quiet at night—" Jimmy picks up his mom's sentence.

"'—and you never know who creeps in the silence.' Yeah, I know, Mom. Don't worry, I'll be fine." He never understood his mom's obsession with the silence. He understood that bobcats and coyotes were nocturnal and silent, but he's been exploring these woods for so long that nothing was going to get him. He looks back over at his parents, concern sinking in his gut. Shrugging, he turns and continues his previous path; they can handle themselves.

Jimmy reaches the screen door and pushes it open, letting it slam shut behind him. Now free from the house, he bolts, his bare feet slamming into the grass with each step. He keeps running, running, running, heading towards the dirt trail that he travels so often. Now he's running on the trail, the trail which leads him to his sanctuary and his escape, where the greenery hides him away from all of Mom's weird warnings and Dad's awkward and constant concern. Run, run, run, then stop. Out of breath and panting, Jimmy walks off the dirt path and into the embrace of his paradise, his kingdom, and his freedom.

A good while later, the blazing ball of light starts shifting from the north and falling towards the opposite direction, the light bouncing off the nearby pond. The green water shimmered, reflecting the young boy's face on the shiny surface. Jimmy always enjoyed staring at the swamp water, but today the pond seemed more still than normal. Not only that, but the trees seemed quieter, too. The constant ruffle of leaves is missing from the normal outdoor symphony. Jimmy stands up, stretching out his arms in the air. He's been outside for a while now and he was hungry, he forgot to pack any food. Jimmy often lost track of time, spending most of it here sitting on the big boulder right next to the pond that he's claimed as his spot. It's his throne, in a kind of way, looking over the forest and the pond. He watches, finishing the last of his stretches, as a frog hops onto his throne, sunbathing in the afternoon light.

"Your name shall be Hopper," he proclaims, pointing towards the frog. Jimmy had to make sure that all his royal subjects were properly accounted for and named. He has named tons of his subjects since the first moment of his reign. He's named fish, frogs, crickets, birds, and any other animal that entered his domain.

Jimmy also realistically knew that multiple "subjects" have probably been renamed a couple of times and there was no tangible way to keep track of each individual animal. That didn't matter though, as far as he was concerned, each animal that's been renamed was just another added to his list of subjects on his mighty land. As of now, his kingdom was flourishing with life and a countless number of peasants that were blessed with a name.

Jimmy started walking towards his new subject Hopper, scanning his slimy brown body over. Hopper is a big frog, the biggest he has seen in a while. Jimmy kept walking towards Hopper, rolling up on the toes of his feet, trying to avoid stepping on any leaves or sticks. It wouldn't do if Hopper hopped off! Jimmy is almost to him when—*plop*, Hopper jumps into the swampy pond.

"Oh well. Maybe I'll catch you next time you lowly subject!" He giggled at his proclamation, the sound echoing off the different trees. It was a shame he couldn't catch Hopper, but he knew it was only a matter of time until Hopper came back. Besides, he didn't really want to be covered in frog slim or frog pee before he went home to eat.

Jimmy stands there next to his next to the now vacated boulder, trying to absorb everything around him. There's that silence again, pressing down. He imagines it feels like a barn cat sitting on a rodent it has caught. Everything around him is too quiet. Jimmy looks up into the pine and oak trees. Normally, he'd be able to spot at least a dozen critters running around and making a ruckus, but not right now. There're not any squirrels, squirming around picking acorns and running other squirrels off, or birds, fighting the squirrels for any berries they might find and just simply singing in the branches. There's not even a praying mantis, walking in its weird way across the canopy, being the menaces they are. Yet, when he looks up now, he sees nothing. Not a squirrel, a bird, a bug, or any other creature in the trees. It's odd and Jimmy doesn't like it. The woods should never be silent.

Jimmy walks the rest of the distance from his throne to the pond, looking over into it. He can see the fish swimming around, stirring up the algae and silt behind them. They look peaceful in the water. The water acts as a different dimension, one in which the outside world has trouble intruding on. Still, even the water was too calm, and the little fish were not doing much to the make noise or waves. Jimmy reaches down, picking up some loose pebbles from the dirt around his feet. He holds out the rocks he just gathered in his open hand and stares, thinking. There was an acorn in the mix of rocks, its presence hiding behind the bigger stones. He always thought that it was interesting how an acorn from so high up like the treetops, could fall to such a low and dirty place as the ground, causing the rocks and acorns to mix with each other. Jimmy looks up from his hand and closes it. With his pondering finished, he tosses the handful of mostly stones into the pond, disrupting the surface. That was better, he thought. Not so silent, not so still. Jimmy reaches back down and picks up another handful of stones, careful to not grab anymore acorns, then places them in the worn front pocket of his overalls.

"Just in case," he says. He was almost positive that there weren't any more water surfaces that needed to be broken on his journey back home, but throwing things is always fun and one can never really be too sure. Jimmy turns away from his pond, his throne, and his humble subjects, back towards the path to his house. He starts out on his trek with rocks in his pocket and a twig he found earlier in hand that he drags behind him, leaving a line in the dirt behind him, a line that someone could probably follow.

He was walking this time, instead of running. Moving slow enough this time that he could actually feel each thorn, leaf, and sharp twig that he was stepping on. Jimmy is on the same trail he took to get to his kingdom in the first place, the trail that was going to bring him home sooner than he liked. Yet, despite the confidence of his path, something feels unsettling. He's walked this trail countless times, but none of them had felt like this. The eerie silence seems to follow Jimmy out of the woods. It clings to his heels, warning of something coming. Even as the woods thinned, the silence did not.

Now at the end of the trail, Jimmy looks over across the vast yard towards his house, painted sky blue and dandelion yellow. Mom chose those colors when his parents had first moved in, Dad objected, but no one wins against Mom when she's had her mind made up. He shifts his eyes and glances over the shaggy brown barn and Aunt Mary's orange tree right next to it, both to the left of his house. Aunt Mary had planted that orange tree there 14 years ago when she was still living here with Mom and Dad, tending to that tree like a small child. No one was ever really sure what happened to Aunt Mary; they all woke up one day and she was just gone.

"Ran away," his dad would say. "She probably left, thinking she could actually make money off all those fancy mystery novels she loved. She said once that she wanted to see the world, so she could capture the world in a book. Nonsense I say, she's probably dead in some strange back alley halfway across the country by now." That was his father's thoughts on Aunt Mary's disappearance; he didn't believe or enjoy all the "mystery nonsense" they say she was always going on about. Jimmy had never known her, but based off the stories he's been told, he's sure he would have liked her at least as much as he likes her orange tree. Done admiring, he looks over from the tree back to the house. This is all Mom and Dad's kingdom, and maybe one day his kingdom will grow from swamp and woods to a house and barn too.

Jimmy drops his stick and starts forward again, finishing his pursuit forward from the trail and towards the chance of food. Walking through the clearing and up onto the porch, Jimmy halts. Something felt very, very, wrong. Reaching for the handle, Jimmy pulls open the screen door and peeks his head into the kitchen. That's odd, Mom wasn't there. Normally by now she would be prepping for dinner, either baking, boiling, or doing dishes at the very least. Jimmy steps into the house. There's an abandoned loaf of bread on the island table, still steaming and fresh.

"Mom! Mom, where are you?" Jimmy keeps moving deeper into the house. He was sure that his mom was going to shout at him for forgetting to bring a lunch, but now he's the one shouting after her. Jimmy kept pressing forward through the kitchen and into the attached living room. No one was here either, but just like in the kitchen, everything looked abandoned, as if time had frozen for a moment. He can see Dad's evening beer on the coffee table and that evening's football match still running on the old TV. But there's something else, something that's not supposed to be here, that quiet stillness. It's odd, unusual, and upsetting, the loud announcer of the game wasn't even able to cut through this suffocating silence. Jimmy rushes out the living room, and to the hallway frantically looking through each room, the bathroom, the bedroom, the office. His parents are nowhere to be found and with each room he searched and didn't find anything, an added layer of doom piled on top of him.

"Mom! Dad! Please! Please come out!" Jimmy stands in the last room, his parents' bedroom, crying with snot running down his face and his clothes drenched in tears. This is the last room they could have been hiding in, the last room that they weren't in. The only other place on the property to look for them is in the barn, the place where they like to hangout. They occasionally meet there with their friends, people he normally never knows, and have meetups, talking about strange things he has yet to fully understand.

Breathing slowly in and out calming himself, Jimmy walks out of the bedroom and back into the hallway, hiccupping all the while as he holds back tears. Jimmy keeps walking through the hallway and as he does, its old, dingy, sunflower wallpaper, stares at him. Each sunflower head begins morphing into the head of a human, judging, and arching over him. Everything is falling in on itself. His world is collapsing with each step he takes. Jimmy starts to run down the hallway and away from all those faces. He sprints through the kitchen, back out the screen door, and starts out towards the barn and Aunt Mary's orange tree. He runs and runs, running as fast as he can. He runs fast enough to try and catch the remnants of his parents or hopefully even them.

Jimmy reaches the barn and slides to a stop, tearing up the grass with his feet and stares up at the aged doors blocking him from going inside. The handles on the doors are old and worn, rusty where they have aged with the white paint peeling on the trim. He remembers always being fussed at when he was younger for peeling that paint off, making the barn look even worse than it already did. He doesn't peel it anymore, though the thought does still occasionally cross his mind and tempt him. Jimmy stays standing at the entrance, glancing up at the sky. The sky is so blue and pretty with fluffy, white clouds lazily floating by. If only it was raining, pouring. If only everything else matched the storm raging through him right now. He knows that this is his last chance. If they aren't here, they were gone, taken by whatever has been haunting over their lives.

Jimmy breathes in a large breath to stop his hiccupping, levels his gaze with the handles, and pulls both barn doors open. The doors creak with the strain of movement, but that was the only sound present. There was nothing, nothing but the horrible quiet settling back down. The barn is as it always was. The tools on the meeting table in a corner under the large hay loft, and particle hay dust floating on the air, glittering with each stray sunbeam they catch. He traces his eyes over those stray beams, starting from a crack in the wall and ending on the floor, landing firmly on Cat. Cat, their gray tabby barn cat, stands up from his sunbathing and starts walking towards Jimmy in greeting. In doing so, Cat reveals that something underneath him. Jimmy walks over to investigate what he was lying on. It wasn't unusual for Cat to lay on random objects, but this item was odd and too small to be a normal feed sack he makes his beds out of. Jimmy catches his breath and freezes. Right in the middle of the breezeway, with that large beam of sunlight he was watching earlier highlighting its existence, is a letter. Jimmy bolts over to it and swipes the letter up, scaring Cat in the process. The letter is old and aged, with a blue wax seal that has an impression of a lily in it, holding it shut. Without a second thought, he rips it open and discards the envelope, quickly trying to read whatever message was left.

In the center of the paper, written with fancy handwriting and black ink, there are four little words. They read, "Don't Trust the Silence," but that wasn't all. In the bottom left corner of the paper, placed like a signature signing off, was a picture of an orange. It's a mandarin and ripe, like the kind off Aunt Mary's orange tree in the fall...

The Entity
Aaron Cloud

I saw it. I heard it. It was there. It was a few months ago, late winter. One of the last calls I ever went out on before I left the department. An apartment complex in the inner city had caught fire. Many of the residents, especially in the upper story, needed to be escorted to safety. I would come to find a young girl stuck up there, she must have been about sixteen, the age of my daughter. It was when I saw her when I encountered the entity. That's what I call it, anyway, for lack of a better term.

After sprinting up the steps, I opened the door of her Family's apartment. There I saw her, trapped amidst the flames in the corner of the room. Fallen debris had pinned her down and crushed her legs. I wish that was the worst of it. There was this abnormal shadow that engulfed the area around her. There was nothing creating it, it was just there. The shadow diverged, making it look like the legs of a colossal spider intent on entangling her. At the same time, disorderly whispers began to swell up inside my mind. I could hear them just as clearly as I could hear the fire alarm ringing on and off across the building, yet I couldn't tell where they were coming from. However strange, though, I had to push these anomalies to the back of my mind as best as I could. This girl's life came first. As her home burned around her, I quickly made my way over to her, tossing the rubble that covered her aside and throwing her over my shoulder. She wasn't crying out during any of this, which initially made it hard to find her when I first entered the room. She must have been unconscious, or at least pretty damn close. She didn't respond when I called out to her either, assuring her she'd be okay.

As I watched the flames adorn the old furniture in the living room and wipe away the memories from the family photos hanging on the wall, I carried her out the front door. The truck's hose had made its assault on the flames in my general direction, making the extraction easier. When I got her down to the rest of the response team, I lowered her from my shoulders and held her in both arms. I hadn't gotten a look at how horribly the flames had mangled her, but I could see it then as I gazed upon her face. Whatever she looked like before was scarred beyond recognition. I couldn't help but stare as my knees began to feel weak. Just then, her face began to reshape itself, and before I knew it, the whispers, those damn whispers came back as well. Suddenly, I was looking down at my own daughter, Sienna. From the long black bangs that made their way almost as far down as her eyes, and the blank, stoic expression she always wore, it was her down to the letter. I stood there, frozen, as I tried to discern what the hell was going on. The whispers didn't help, either. "Banks? Banks?" one of my comrades called out. I don't know how long I just stood there for, but I guess it was long enough for them to notice. "It's alright, I'll take her from here." I hadn't looked up to see who it was, and the whispers made it difficult to tell by his voice, but whoever it was gently took her from my arms and brought her to the ambulance.

I couldn't do my job anymore after that night. I had gone on a few more calls, but I froze each time. That young girl supposedly passed away in the hospital later in the night, which hadn't made things easier for me. I couldn't just shake off what had happened like I had done for almost two decades before. I was effectively useless to my comrades, so I decided to leave. I still live with my wife and daughter, who are happy to support me even though I'm unable to work. They know I've undergone some kind of trauma, but I haven't given them the specifics, especially not about the entity. They'd call me crazy if they knew. I guess anyone would. But I wasn't crazy. That thing, whatever it is, made itself known to me. I wasn't going to pretend to know how this thing operated or how its mind worked, but I had a pretty solid guess. It had attached itself to me. It must have. And it couldn't have shown me Sienna's face on accident. No, that was deliberate. It was a warning. She was next. I knew I had to kill this thing before it could follow through on its threat, even if it was some kind of demon, even if it was Satan himself, I would send it back to hell.

...

A few months after the incident, I found myself shifting through the aisles of a Home Depot almost mindlessly. I had allowed my facial hair to grow after I quit, no longer needing to be clean shaven for my job. I still wasn't used to it, it was uncomfortable, and yet I never bothered to shave it anymore. The store's fluorescent lights beamed down on me as I passed the shelves. That was uncomfortable too. This whole damn empty place was uncomfortable. Even the orange paint got on my nerves. I couldn't say what was taking me so long. I don't know what Dr. Morrow would say either. He was the psychiatrist I started seeing at my wife, Esther's, insistence. I went a few times, and I let a few things slip about that night, but I never saw him again after that, though Esther doesn't know about that. I had never been an advocate for therapy, and if you ask me, Dr. Morrow only served to prove my point. The way he talked and the words he would use pissed me off. He wouldn't be able to help me with anything I need him to, anyway. I doubt his books and degrees would be any use against what I was fighting.

After looking through the store's inventory for a little while, I found what I needed. A standard red gas can with a black spout, able to hold two gallons.

"Evening, sir! Will that be all for you?" A skinny college aged young man greeted me at the register with a smile on his face.

"Yeah," I replied blanky

"Eighteen Eighty-Eight," he said, motioning to the card reader.

"I'll pay in cash," I said, still not reciprocating his smile. After awkwardly fumbling through my wallet, I handed him a twenty-dollar bill.

"Alrighty, let me get your change for you, sir."

"Don't bother." I had already turned to face the door by then.

"Well then, you have a nice night, sir! Going somewhere far, I take it?"

"What?" I said sharply as I turned back around. I looked at him like he had just asked me the dumbest question he could have possibly fathomed, though I quickly realized it made sense that he thought that.

"I said, you going somewhere far?"

My expression relaxed once again. "No," I replied, and turned back around.

"Oh, ok. Well, take care, then!"

"You too, bud," I said, barely moving my lips as I made my way to the exit.

I got in my truck, tossing the can into the back seat. I closed my eyes and took a deep breath. This small respite was probably all the rest that I'd be getting these next few hours. As I opened my eyes again to start the engine, I saw a tiny humanoid creature with the wings of a dragonfly sitting atop my steering wheel. I screamed as my whole body pressed back against my seat.

"Hi, I'm Tib!" the thing said, seemingly unbothered. Sure enough, it was a damn fairy. He sat nude on top of my steering wheel. His skin was lime green, and his silver hair was sleeked to the side. He looked like he had jumped straight out of movie, and yet, at the seam time, he was as real as the liquor in my cupholder.

"What?! What the fuck?" I wheezed, trying to collect my breath.

"It's ok, Tib is friendly! Tib isn't mean!" the creature tried to assure me. His voice was irritatingly high pitched, and he structured his speech as if he were a child.

"Ok, ok," I said, calmer than I was a few seconds ago. I already had my encounter with the entity, after all. I supposed If a thing like that could exist, then this wasn't quite as strange. "What the hell are you doing in my car, Tib?"

"Tib wants to know your name! What's your name?"

I sighed, massaging my temples with my index finger and thumb. He had the mindset of a toddler, after all. I figured I would have to just play his game. "Damien. Damien Banks."

"Damien! Damien! Damien!" The thing repeated gleefully, hopping up and down off of his rear end.

I exhaled heavily. This was turning into an excruciatingly long night. "Yeah. That's my name. You got it. Now tell me why you're in my truck."

"Tib wants to be friends! And your house looks nice!"

"My house? No, Tib, I don't live in here, it's a —" I stopped myself. Listen to me, I was actually trying to reason with this fairy. "Listen, Tib. Could you just... leave? I can roll down the window for you, or whatever." Just then the thought occurred to me, how exactly did he get in here?

Tib crossed his arms and glared at me with his surprisingly large eyes, at least compared to the rest of his body. "Damien doesn't want to be friends with Tib? Why not?"

I sighed and tried to make myself sound as polite as humanly possible. "Surely, you can go make some other friends, right? You seem like a sociable little guy."

"No!" he raised his voice, "Tib wants to be friends with Damien!"

I closed my eyes again and rubbed my face. Why not humor him, I decided? He couldn't be that dangerous, and it's not like he was in the mood to negotiate. "Fine, Tib. We can be friends. Just get up and move somewhere else so I can steer, alright? I have to get moving."

His face lit up. "Ok, Damien!" He flew from the wheel and onto my shoulder. Damnit, he was attached to me already.

I started the ignition, put the truck in gear, and began turning out of the parking lot. Tib had a puzzled look on his face, like the absolute last thing he expected this thing to do was move. As I got onto the highway and sped up, poor Tib had been blown off my shoulder and was now clutching the headrest as best he could with his little hands. "What are you doing, Damien?" he asked, clearly concerned.

"I'm going home."

"But you're already in here!"

"No, Tib, I already told you — damn it, never mind."

After a few miles, I had turned off from the highway and the truck was at a more moderate speed. Tib was more comfortable now, and he was fiddling around in the backseat. He straddled the spout of the gas can. "What's this for, Damien?"

"That? It holds gas, Tib."

"Gas? What's the gas for?"

I thought about it for a moment. How was I supposed to explain what I had planned to anyone, let alone a fairy with the mental capacity of a newborn puppy? Then again, maybe Tib would understand better than anyone. Maybe he and the entity were cut from the same cloth. "What do know about spirits, Tib?"

"Spirits? Tib isn't a spirit. Tib is a fairy!"

"I know that Tib, but you have some sort of otherworldly air about you. Maybe you've delt with something of the sort. A spirit, or, I don't know, a ghost maybe? A demon?"

"Nope! Nuh uh!"

I sighed in disappointment. "It was worth a shot, I guess."

"Why does Damien want to know?" He looked up at me, hanging from the middle compartment with both hands.

"I had a run in with one."

"You did? When?" His wings fluttered. Maybe that was akin to a dog wagging its tail. I wasn't sure.

"Back when I was still a firefighter."

"A firefighter? What's that?" He really was like a child. I was being accosted with question after question.

"What the hell does it sound like it is, Tib?"

Tib's wings fluttered again, this time more rapidly. "Hey! That was mean! Are all humans mean?"

"Fuck off," I responded in an attempt to answer his question.

The rest of the drive was more of the same. Tib would pester me with what I thought were stupid questions, and I would answer them with some snarky remark. It occurred to me that maybe my attitude would rub off on him, but I didn't really care. I stopped by a gas station on the way home to fill the can.

...

Eventually, we pulled into the driveway of my home. It wasn't anything too crazy. Only one story and it didn't take up too much space, but it had a nice, solid brick foundation and it wasn't too rough to look at. The location wasn't so bad, either. A pleasant neighborhood in a comely Houston suburb. It was springtime too. If there was any green to be seen in Houston, then I imagine it would have been green and lively here.

I turned the ignition off as the garage door closed behind me. I turned to Tib, "Stay in the truck. If you go anywhere near my family, I'll rip your wings off and feed them to you." I did reluctantly agree to be his "friend" to placate him, but truth be told. I was already sick of him by now.

"Fine, fine. TIb will stay in the truck." He crossed his arms and defiantly turned his gaze away from me. He was stubborn as usual, but my threat worked.

I stepped out of the truck; the humid garage instantly made me feel at home. It wasn't too often these days I got to enjoy how that felt. It was like entering some divine sanctuary. It seemed as if all I had to do was open the door in front of me and there would be a sprawling hot bath across the floor. I let the heavenly feeling sit for a moment. When I finally grounded myself and opened the door, it wasn't a bathhouse waiting for me. Instead, it was Sienna sitting on the couch in her pajamas, a blanket wrapped around her with a PlayStation controller in her hands.

Her expression was stern and concentrated on the Television screen when I walked in. When she noticed me, her eyes widened, and her mouth opened ever so slightly. "Hey, Dad," she said mid-breath. Evidentially my visit was a surprise.

"Hey, kid," I said back, closing the door behind me. "Does Mom know you're up this late?"

"No. Don't tell her, please," she said laxly as her face shifted into a small grin, as if she knew I wouldn't. Easy enough, I guessed. There was plenty worse I hadn't been telling Esther as of late. "How have you been? You haven't been home a lot. Are you ok?"

"I'm fine," I replied, joining her on the couch. "Everything will get sorted out in time." Coming home this late felt the same way it used to when I would stay at the station overnight. Many of those nights were not so dissimilar to tonight, where I found Sienna waiting in the living room playing some game or another.

Sometimes she'd interrupt herself to hug me, even in my dirty work clothes. I suppose she was too focused on whatever she was doing tonight, though. I took a moment to take in what was laid before me on the flat screen TV. I saw what I assumed was my daughter's avatar, who was dressed like a knight. He was engaged in combat with another armored man who towered over him. "What are you playing?" I asked.

"Dark Souls," she responded, her eyes still locked on the screen. "I've been stuck on this boss for the past few hours."

"Past few hours? Don't you have school in the morning?"

"No, Dad, it's Friday," she said. Her attention was too centered on the game to convey any emotion.

"Huh, I guess it is." I hadn't really known. These past few months, whatever day of the week it happened to be was entirely inconsequential to me. "So that's the guy you're stuck on?" I asked, referring to the large figure adorned in what I could now tell were priestly robes. The two had been battling in what looked like a church, or rather a cathedral judging by its scale. Her foe held two swords, one of which was engulfed in flames, while the other had an ethereal purple glow to it, while her knight was armed with only a steel shield and a mace.

"Yeah, Pontiff Sulyvahn. He's a prick."

"Odd name," I commented. It sounded like she was speaking a foreign language to me. Everything about her game seemed foreign. "Why's he so big?" I asked, to which she just shrugged. He moved quickly towards her character, and even swung his blades, which looked to be taller than the knight's entire body, swiftly and effortlessly. "Doesn't seem like a fair fight," I added.

"It's not supposed to be fair; that's the point."

"Beats me," I shrugged. Though he moved with an impossible swiftness and must have been at least thrice her size, she was ready for just about every move he made. There must have been a rhythm to it that she had figured out. "Looks like you're winning though."

She sighed, "This is only the first part. Once you get him low enough, he summons a clone of himself to help him fight you."

"Well damn, how do you beat that?"

"I don't know, I'm still figuring that out," she said with a hint of exhaustion in her voice. My fatherly instincts told me to put my arm around her, but I didn't want to break her concentration, so I sat there with my hands in my pockets.

I watched her contest with the pontiff a little while longer. I even saw the clone she talked about. It was a nice rest at first, but then it became eerie, as I realized how all too similar it was to the thoughts that had been racing through my mind all day. The confrontation with some monstrous figure, the flames on his sword, a sense of human resilience, even the atmosphere of the battle. I'm not one to believe in universal signs or causality, but it seemed like I was meant to see this. After the conflict started to seem redundant to me, I got up. "Listen, kiddo. My axe from the station is still sitting in the kitchen. I've got to go return it."

She finally turned her attention away from the screen and to me. Apparently, what I had just said bewildered her. "Now? But it's like, two in the morning, Dad." I was almost disappointed in her, even angry that she took her attention away from her fight with Pontiff Sulyvahn. The realization struck me that I was actually invested in that game of hers, to my surprise. I wanted her to put that son of a bitch in his place. It felt like she was just a kid again playing little league soft ball, as she struck out because she was too busy waving at her mother and I in the bleachers instead of watching the ball.

"It'll be fine. There's always someone at the station. I'll be back soon."

"Please just stay, Dad. You're never here anymore, and you haven't even been home for ten minutes yet. You can take it in the morning," she said with blaring concern written all over her face and frustration in her voice. "I don't even know what you do when you're not here. You're starting to worry me."

82

"You're too young to be worrying about your old man like that. I told you it won't be long."

"Ok," she said, though I could tell by the sadness in her voice she wasn't convinced. "Be safe, Dad." It was more of a plea than the usual formality.

I nodded. "Get to bed soon, ok?" She nodded back.

I made my way to the kitchen, which could almost be considered the same room as the living room. There were no walls or doors separating the two, and the living room even had the same tiled floor as the kitchen instead of a carpet. I grabbed my fire axe, which I had previously placed in front of a few cupboards under the counter that nobody ever opened.

With the axe resting on my shoulder, I started walking back to the garage door. I took one last look at Sienna. "Hey," I said as she turned toward me again. "Kick that guy's ass for me."

"I'll try," she smiled.

I smiled contentedly. I went back into the garage. Before I could open the door to my truck, Tib surprised me, floating just above my head. "Who were you talking to in there?" he asked.

I quickly pointed my gaze up at him. That little pixie had already soured my mood. "What does it matter, Tib? I told you to stay in the truck and away from my family."

"So, you were talking to your family, then?" he continued.

I sighed, annoyed. "Yeah, my daughter."

"Is she mean like you?" he demanded, his tone louder, not missing a beat.

"Shut up, Tib." I answered. "Get in the truck or get the hell out of here. I don't care which."

Tib frowned as he uncrossed his arms and let them hang down. "I'm sorry, Damien," he said, a sense of regret decorating his tone. I didn't even know his infantile brain could feel regret. "I don't really think you're mean, not actually. I heard the way you talked to her. You wouldn't have talked to her that way if you were mean."

I couldn't believe what I was hearing. Was he speaking articulately for the first time? And did he just refer to himself in first person? More importantly, I couldn't believe what I was feeling. Had this little fairy, who had been nothing but a thorn in my side since I met him, actually touched my heart? Of course, he appealed to my fatherhood. What a low blow. Nevertheless, I lowered my guard just as he had. "Thanks, Tib," I said softly. I opened the door to the truck. "You coming?"

Tib happily flew right in, and I followed behind him. Still, his words stuck with me. Suddenly, they weren't as comforting as they had been just a few moments ago. Maybe I was mean, I thought. I had lied to her, after all. I don't think Tib even picked up on that. I had absolutely zero intent of going to the station. I had grabbed my axe for another reason entirely, the same reason I procured the can of gas earlier in the night. I pressed a button on my cell phone to open the garage door and backed out, closing it once more as I started towards my destination.

...

I sat anxiously in the driver's seat, both hands clasping the wheel, though I wasn't moving. Before me stood the once proud Harmony Creek First Baptist Church, or at least what was left of it. I used to drive by it all the time. It was once the center of a thriving community, but those times had long passed. It had been foreclosed years ago, after a hurricane had devastated most of the surrounding residences. It hadn't been looked after since. There was good news for me, though. Nobody was around, which meant what I was about to do had no risk of hurting anyone other than myself. I took a quick breath, and with my eyes closed, turned the ignition of the truck off, as if I was afraid to look for some reason. Once out of the truck, I made my way through the tall blades of the ugly, uncut grass, the axe in one hand and the gas can in the other.

"What are you doing, Damien?" Tib asked impatiently.

"I'm trying to summon it."

"Summon what? Summon what?" He buzzed around. I was more accepting of his childlike attitude by now.

"Remember the thing I told you about?"

"Ohhhh, oh yeah, I think I remember!"

"I first saw it in a fire. I'm no expert on the occult, but I figure if I start another fire, it'll show itself again. Especially since it has a history with me."

"Oh, fire! Sounds fun!" Tib exclaimed. How could he be so mindful in one instance and so damn careless in the next?

"It won't be fun; I don't even know how to kill this thing. I have to try, though."

At this point in the conversation, I had made it to the double doors of the entrance. I kicked the right door in with ease. It was far from the sturdiest door I had to break through in my time. The place was dark and damp, as expected. The hurricane hadn't managed to knock it over, but most of the wood that made up the walls was rotted, and there were a few holes to be found in it. All I could do was hope it would stay up long enough for me to do what I needed to do. I began pouring gasoline across the diameter of the church, mainly around the walls and the support beams between the two collum's of pews. Tib watched in anticipation as I took a few deep breaths, then lit a match and threw it onto the path of gasoline I had left. I was now holding the Axe in both hands, as I waited for the flames to spread to the rest of the building. "Come out, damn it," I murmured. "I know you want to."

The wait felt endless, but the flames that surrounded me grew stronger and stronger. Suddenly, a black mist filled the air around me. Though there was a roof above my head, I felt as if I was watching the sky itself go dark. There, atop the steps at the end of the hall, in front of the lectern, the shadows began to consolidate into a single slim figure. That was it, that was the entity. There could be no doubt. It had made itself known again. Its form was still ambiguous like before. I couldn't even make out the shadows all the way. But the whispers had begun again, the whispers that I couldn't quite decipher. That's how I knew it was my old foe.

"Yes, there you are," I raised my axe in the air and charged towards it. I only got a few steps forward before the entity had hellishly dashed towards me and was right in front of my face. Whatever semblance of a form that it had disintegrated as more shadows appeared and encircled me. The shadows began twirling around me as they grew taller. Damnit, it was already toying with me. As if to tell me that I stood no shot. The shadows, still dancing in a wall around me, made it all the way to my neck before I could work up the nerve to do something about it. I desperately swung my axe at the dark mist encompassing me, and sure enough, it disappeared. The entity, however, was far from defeated. In fact, I doubt I had even phased it. It was only testing me. Testing my will to fight. It reappeared right in front of me, taking on the most discernable form it ever had up to this point. In front of me was a mirror image. It was me. Just as the entity had copied Sienna's appearance before, now it was echoing me, and I saw just how disheveled I had become in the past few months. My hair, which I had styled in a mid-part, was as long as I've ever seen it before. My beard was entirely unkempt, and it was evident that I had gained weight too. I would not let this phase me; I was growing used to the entity's tricks. It smiled at me. Even though its teeth were a reflection of mine, they looked so unsettling. It raised its arms, giving me an invitation to strike. Screaming, I raised my axe and attempted to bury it in the foul things neck. Right as the blade made contact, it disappeared again. The flames around me began changing color. Green, now red again, now blue. The entity had gone into hiding, if you could call it that. But its presence was still obvious. It made sure of that.

"Show yourself!' I shouted. "Come out!" I started swinging my axe wildly and ending up cutting into one of the support pillars. My voice was distorted by rage "I'll make you suffer! I'll make you suffer like you made that girl suffer!"

Right at that moment, I heard Tib shout. I had forgotten about him. "Damien, right above you!" I looked up, as I saw a flaming wood beam falling right on top of me. I quickly rolled out of the way, as the beam landed behind me.

"Good call, Tib!" I shouted back. I looked around for the entity, and after a moment, I had my sights on it. It was once again in front of the lectern, back in its slim shadowy form. But this time, oddly, it had a teethy smile, just like it did when it took on my appearance. Its chin was tilted upward. It was mocking me, looking down on me, the large wooden cross burning behind it.

Just then, a watery mist fell over the church as the flames began to die down. What the hell was happening? I looked to the left, and out from a gaping hole in the wall I could see a sight I knew far too well. It was a firetruck. The water was coming from the deck gun. Damn it, how long had I taken? I had to wrap this up now, it was the only way I could ensure my family's safety. One more time, I raced towards the entity at the head of the church. I ran up the stairs, throwing my axe around with a flurry of swings. This time, the entity remained still when I approached it, but I still couldn't make it feel any pain. It fell back after every swing. Each time my axe lacerated a part of its body it would just disappear then reappear unharmed. I didn't know how long this went on for before I heard a voice coming from the front door.

"Mr. Banks? Mr. Banks? Please calm down. My name is David Cross. I'm a crisis intervention specialist. I'm here to help. Please, follow me outside where it's safe." I turned to see a stocky man with a shaven head, dressed in khakis and short sleeved white button up shirt. Around his neck his was a lanyard holding some sort of identification. Accompanying him was a host of police officers, who stayed a safe distance behind him.

"Stay back! don't you realize how important this is? Stay back, damn it!" I shouted as the man proceeded forward. "I'm fucking serious, stay back! It's laughing at us!"

"Mr. Banks, please. I am a mental health professional. We have reason to believe you are not in your right mind. Please, put the weapon down and let us talk this out."

My only instinct was to keep swinging my axe around, which brought the man to a halt. "It's laughing at us! Don't you get it? It's laughing at us! It's laughing at me!"

"Mr. Banks, you need to come with me. Your family is greatly concerned about you and your behavior as of late."

"My family? How do you know anything about my family?" I demanded. Just as the words had left my mouth, I felt a cold chill across my entire body. It was the entity's turn to strike. I turned around to counter it, and I felt a shock travel through me as I fell to the ground and dropped my axe. I laid there motionless. Just as I was starting to gain movement again, three sets of arms and legs pinned me to the ground. I fought against them as best I could. I tried to wrench myself free as they held a hand behind my back. I could still see the entity standing above me. With tears brought upon by pure anger obscuring my vision, I reached for my axe with my free hand. I grunted, and it smiled down at me with that disgusting mouth it had. Before I could grab the handle, one of the officers forced my hand behind my back with the other one as they restrained me with a zip tie.

They forced me up on my feet, turned me around, and began walking me back to the front door, though I fought them every literal step of the way. At that moment, it had come to my attention that I could not see Tib nor the entity. Where had they gone? The entity knew how to conceal itself, and Tib could have easily flown away when the authorities showed up. It's not inconceivable that they're both in hiding. But what if that man, David Cross he said his name was, was telling the truth? What if I wasn't even in control over my own mind anymore? No, it couldn't be. The entity had deliberately picked a fight with me. This isn't something that David Cross, Dr. Morrow, Sienna, or Esther could possibly understand. It made itself known to me, and only me, for whatever reason. Oh, Cross, if only it was as simple as you say it is. For a moment, just for a moment, I questioned if any if it was real. In that moment, as the police forced me to the door and Cross watched on with a frown on his face, I saw it yet again, standing at the door as they dragged me out, cackling to itself as it watched me struggle in vain.

Beautiful Stranger
Gabriela Valiente

When Ryley first sees her, she doesn't think twice of it ... no, that's a lie. She thinks of it more than twice. She has to stop what she's doing at the little coffee shop in town and stare at the beautiful brown-haired woman that just walked in.

She isn't the only one, either. Everyone seems to be struck by her appearance. It's as if time has stopped and the only thing moving is her.

Ryley has to quickly avert her eyes when the woman passes her to get to the counter. It's then that her senses get filled with her scent and wow, she thinks. She smells just as lovely as she looks.

She waits a moment before looking up and she freezes. A pair of huge, brown eyes are looking back at her and Ryley suddenly gets an ache in her chest. They seem to carry so much sadness, and she doesn't understand why. She wishes she could do something—say something, at least—but it's all too much. She has to tear her gaze away.

She doesn't look up until she hears the barista call out a name.

Astrid.

Ryley smiles as she watches the woman get her drink and leave the building.

What a beautiful name for a beautiful person.

-

When Ryley sees her—Astrid—again, it's the only thing she thinks about. She's at the train station, getting off at her usual stop for work. This time it's different, however, because she suddenly sees a bundle of brown, curly hair heading towards the train.

She stops, unsure of how to react. Weeks of confusing Astrid with every brunette on the street has taught Ryley to not act on her impulses. But this doesn't feel like another mistake.

She feels a pair of eyes on her and the way her chest swells tells her it's the same ones that have been at the forefront of her mind. She turns around and there she is, staring back at her.

Ryley doesn't want to waste this opportunity. She makes her way back onto the train, ignoring complaints as she pushes past bodies, but it's too late. The doors close and with that her chance to speak to Astrid.

-

Ryley is restless. It's been months since she saw Astrid at the train station. Retracing her steps in hopes of finding her have been to no avail. At this point, she's afraid it's all been a part of her imagination, a cruel but beautiful trick.

Her despair must have been apparent on her face because Luca, her closest friend, points it out during their weekly dinner outing.

"Hey, what's up with you?" he asks, pointing his fork at her. "I'm sensing a lot of ... melancholy."

Ryley contemplates telling him the truth. Not only is she sad about the situation, but she's also embarrassed. She's heartbroken over someone she doesn't even know. "There's this girl..." she ultimately begins but quickly regrets when she sees how excited Luca gets. "It's not like that. I haven't even talked to her."

He raises both brows. "And she has you like this? She clearly made an impression on you."

She gives a single nod, placing her fork on her untouched plate of pasta. "Her eyes, Luca. They're so beautiful. She's so beautiful."

"Do you know her name?"

"Only her first name. Astrid." She holds on to her name—lets the word linger on her lips. It's the only thing she has of her. "I saw her first at a coffee shop, then the train station, but that's it. I haven't seen her in months."

"I would've done a social media search for you, but we're working with nothing."

Although Luca's words are true, they hurt, nonetheless. But, perhaps, she needed to hear them out loud. "It's fine," she sighs. "We were simply meant to pass by each other's lives."

-

The world works in mysterious ways and surprises you when you least expect it. Ryley hasn't been alive long enough to be considered wise, but she knows this to be true when she finally finds Astrid just when she comes to the conclusion that she never will.

It's at a chapel, no less. The last place you would find Ryley in. But it was the anniversary of her mother's passing and she felt the need to be closer to her now more than ever. That's why she's currently knelt down, unsure of what to do with her sweaty hands clasped in front of her.

She isn't drawn to religion the way her mother was, but she loved her very much, so she followed suit every time she went to service. She remembers her closing her eyes and a peacefulness settling over her. Ryley tries to replicate that.

She closes her eyes, tightly at first—her entire body tense,but as the seconds go by, enveloped in darkness, she feels herself relax. It's as if a weight is being taken from her shoulders. She stays like this—not needing to say anything as memories of her mother resurface—until a shuffling next to her brings her back to the present. She becomes aware of her surroundings once again and is deeply embarrassed of the vulnerable state she's caught in.

When she hears the sound of lightning candles, smells the burning scent of incense, she opens her eyes. She needs to blink a couple times to adjust to the dim glow, but when her vision focuses on the figure by her side, all air rushes out of her. "Astrid," she whispers like a prayer.

Ryley is afraid she didn't hear her—or worse, she's afraid it's yet another mind trick with the way the light from the candles cast a halo over her. But Astrid stops murmuring under her breath and opens her eyes. They widen at the sight of Ryley, as if she also can't quite believe what she's seeing. "You."

A single word—barely heard over her beating heart—but it's enough to unravel Ryley. She takes a moment to simply look at Astrid. At her full-length brown curls. At her devastatingly sad and beautiful eyes. She wants to say so much, but she's at a complete loss for words. "I'm Ryley," she eventually says.

Astrid smiles and Ryley is blinded by it. In that moment, in front of all the Gods, she vows to lessen the burdens that rest on her shoulders— that are reflected in her eyes. She deserves to be content,in peace. "It's nice to finally meet you."

—

(Sometime later, Ryley finds herself intertwined with Astrid in the bed of their shared home. She looks down at brown eyes that blink up at her, shining despite the lack of light around them.

Astrid runs her finger over Ryley's cheekbone, her jaw—every part of her face. "I thought you weren't real," she confesses. A whisper in the dark. "When I saw you at the chapel... I thought I had lost it. Even now, I can't help but think that."

Ryley's heart aches. Astrid confessed to her almost every night. Most times, she spoke of the tragedies of her life. The ones that led her to wearing her sorrow as a veil. "I'm real, Astrid," she says, taking her hands and pulling her impossibly closer. She wants her to know—to feel—that her words are true. "This is real.")

The Dead Stranger on My Shelf
Claudia Cooper

On my way home, I spotted a neon yellow yard sign advertising an estate sale. I recognized the address, the street just around the corner from mine, so I took a detour. A dark green canopy marked the house along with a cluster of parked cars. My car soon joined them, my body gravitating to the tables under the shade of the canopy. I smiled at whoever made eye contact, hoping there wasn't a need for polite conversation while perusing a dead person's things. There wasn't anything that interested me at the tables, so I ventured into the house; that's probably where all the good stuff was. Inside, the furniture was homely and dated, arranged as if someone still lived here. There was an emptiness though — in the missing chairs and picture frames. Price tags were stuck to everything that wasn't attached to the house. Once again, nothing was calling out to me, not even the humble three-dollar decorative ashtray where a cigarette would rest between a woman's breasts. Then, I entered the dining room. It housed the perfect vase to fill up the empty spot on my bookshelf. I could picture its place there vividly: the vase's elegant curves contrasting against the harsh, linear lines of my books and its porcelain reflection in the sunlight stream- Calm down. It was just a vase.

Yes, just a vase. One that was shaped like an antique but priced like a knock-off. Fifteen dollars was a steal, even if the vase wasn't as old or as valuable as it looked. Wasting little time, I brought it over to the lady under the canopy outside. We exchanged pleasantries before I handed over the money, and she removed the price tag.

Back home, I noticed the vase was quite dusty, so I grabbed a wet rag to wipe it down. When I got to the inside, it was a tight squeeze to fit my hand through the opening. I couldn't see what was inside, but I could feel it. A lot more dust than there should be. I quickly retracted my hand, fine dust spilling from the rag.

This wasn't what I thought it was, right? I took another look at the vase, surveying the bulbous body and tapered neck. Blue chinoiserie decorated the glossy porcelain, giving nothing away as to what this vase held. Carefully, I tipped the vase over, fine particles, like sand, spilling out into a heap. I brought a shaky, dust-covered hand up to probe at the heap, eventually finding what I was hoping not to. A yellowed tooth.

This was human remains. Not. Dust.

My hand shot out from the heap of ashes to under the faucet, washing away the disgusting and probably hazardous material.

Until I realized this was someone's relative going down the drain. "Crap," I muttered before drying my hands.

Hopefully, the small amount of ashes wouldn't be missed. The bigger pile sitting on my table, however, would. How to go about cleaning it up though? It felt disrespectful to use a broom and dustpan, but it was also the most appropriate. A vacuum wouldn't do and neither would my hands. With most of the ashes collected in the dustpan, I emptied it into a plastic bowl and covered it in saran wrap.

I was still going to keep the vase, but the ashes should go back to the rightful owner. I hurried back to the estate sale, plastic-wrapped bowl in hand. The lady under the canopy seemed confused at my reappearance, but she smiled and greeted me nonetheless. "Hello, again. Is everything alright?"

"Um, hi. That vase you sold me earlier? Well, it's actually an urn." I unwrapped the plastic and tilted the bowl in her direction so she could peek inside. Her eyebrows shot up to her hairline in surprise. "I, uh, think you ought to have these back."

"Oh, I don't want them."

"What? But they're your relatives?"

"No, all my family's buried in the ground. I don't know whose ashes you've got, but it's probably just a pet. Get rid of 'em."

"No, these are human." I emphasize with a shake of the bowl. "There's a molar in here. A very human molar."

"Look, whatever or whoever my mother kept in that vase, I wouldn't know. I haven't talked to her in thirteen years, and I don't intend to keep anything of hers. You bought them, you get to decide what to do with them."

I was stunned into silence, which the lady took as her cue to move on to an actual customer. I looked down at the bowl before sighing, wrapping it back in the plastic. I felt bad for whoever's ashes I was carrying. No one seemed to care about them, at least after that lady's mother died. I took the ashes back home, uncertain of what to do with them.

I could just throw them away or flush them down the toilet. I could spread them in the ocean or in the wind. I could even bury them in my garden; although, I wasn't too keen on using human remains as my fertilizer.

I could do a number of things really, but there was only one suitable option. The moment my eyes set on the antique vase back at home, I decided it would become an urn again. It was foolish of me to even remove the ashes in the first place; the body should never be moved from its final resting place.

Perhaps it was strange to feel empathy for a dead stranger with no face, but I felt they might appreciate the little spot I have for them on my bookshelf.

Past the Living Room
Keely Viator

Its two cute windows on the front exterior peered like eyes into the neighborhood. That's part of what Eliza liked so much about this house. When it was new, she could delight in her face reflected in the tile, and even now, old, the long-worn flooring held a charm in the way it cradled her feet as she walked through the rooms. Living alone in the house, she began to feel it was her duty alone to care for it, keep it clean, and make sure it didn't fall apart beneath her. It really only made sense Eliza would eventually come to carry high hopes of renovating it.

She worked long hours to cultivate these hopes into something real; it was a hard task with only one income. This meant Eliza spent a lot of her free time tired and at home, though, which meant she had plenty of time to think of exactly what she was working towards. As much as she tried to focus on her goal, however, she wasn't the type who could stay alone without other people to talk to in the long term. Luckily for her, that's where coworkers came in. She went out for after-work drinks, attended noisy company parties, and did anything she could to sate a desire for vocal companionship. The house couldn't talk, after all; its thin walls could only listen, if that. It was fine at first. The problems began when she started bringing people home. Most of her friends were friendly, sure. They had a drink, complimented the curtains, and sometimes, if they got comfortable enough, they would sprawl themselves out on the living room couch and open up about their own lives, their own homes. Work wasn't worth the groceries it paid for, the daughter kept peeling the wallpaper, the porch needed redoing—Eliza would listen with a sympathetic ear, rubbing the armrest of her chair with a thoughtful hand. Then she would agreeably comment on how rough that all sounded and pour her guest another drink. They would turn on the television and the discussion would turn towards more pleasant topics about new restaurants opening or what music was currently on one another's mind. That was fine too.

There was one man named Dane who's problems always seemed to go in a certain direction. His house was never clean enough, he hated the pattern of the carpet, and his wife refused to change any of it no matter how much he complained. He would tell Eliza about how he wished he could stay in this nice little house forever, how she kept it spotless despite how hard she worked at her job. He mentioned how much he loved the aged look of the tiles in the kitchen. It was flattering, the way he seemed so eager to compliment his surroundings when he was visiting. He started to come over often, and Eliza would tell him about her renovation ideas.

She wanted to replace the sinks, which were beginning to rust. She wanted to repaint the walls, which were starting to chip and dull. She wanted to make the railing of the stairs, which were starting to give way and creak more and more, safer and more ornate to look at from a distance or close up. It would be cozy, it would be colorful, it would keep that same charm she fell in love with when she first moved in. Those wide-eyed panes that made up the front of the house would be cleaned to translucent brightness, and the inside would show just as much life to it as the outside. Dane sat silent and with closed eyes, taking it all in.

Then he would ask to use the bathroom just past the living room, after which he would raise his arms in a stretch before announcing it was about time to head back to his own home. Eliza would nod and agree, opening the door and allowing him out. She would clean up the living room, then go upstairs to lie on the bed. Staring at the ceiling above like that, it was hard to guess what she could be thinking. She talked less and less aloud to herself as she brought people home that she could talk to instead. She still swept the floor often, though, and she would hum quietly to herself while she did it, turning up the dial on the radio when a song she particularly liked came on. Just like that, the house would be clean in preparation for the next friendly visit.

This became something of a pattern, a routine grown used to. The variety of people dropped, sure, but the frequency of visits started to become more consistent. Sometimes Mila, a friend from before the days of Eliza working so hard, would come; sometimes she'd even bring her children, and the sound of many voices would echo from rooms all the way across the house. The walls were never strong at muffling voices from one room to the next. She seemed to appreciate Eliza's company, though she thought the house a bit old-fashioned for someone as youthfully middle-aged as Eliza to be staying in. She'd ask Eliza about it sometimes, and Eliza would bring up her plans.

However, Mila didn't seem to understand the passion behind the renovation. She'd mention how expensive it could become, especially as the house grew older and more brittle. When that didn't seem to get through, she'd comment on nicer, more manageable houses she'd seen up for sale in the neighborhood, ones that would fit someone single and aspiring like Eliza far better than the one that she currently called home. The pressure grew hurtful, and, sensing that hurt, Mila began to stop bringing her children over. She began to visit less, which only left her comments to settle more solidly through the house. She seemed to think the house was reaching an unsafe point, even if she was scared saying so bluntly would offend those listening. It didn't matter much, either way; whatever damage she could do was already done. Eliza just tried her hardest to keep the counters wiped down, to keep the upholstery clean.

Of course, Dane's compliments during his visits were as uplifting as usual; they gave encouragement that Mila's opinion was not fully objective, that there was hope for this house yet. Sure, sometimes he would track muddy feet across the entrance hall, and occasionally he would spill his drink on the upholstery. There was never any harm meant by it though, and it was clear he respected the home he was a guest in. When Eliza, freshly sensitive, brought up Mila's words, he was quick to reassure that he had no concerns about the house holding up; Eliza planned to improve it, after all, and those improvements would do away with any hazards the house might pose for Eliza or her guests. For now, though, he recommended getting a better television; the images on the screen looked greener than what he watched at home.

Then came the day Dane visited while in a poor mood. It started subtle at first, a small pout that made him look like he was holding breath in his cheeks. Eliza poured him a glass of water, but he refused to touch it where it sat on the coffee table. She asked him what was wrong, and something seemed to finally give. He stood up from the couch and started to rant. His troubles back at his own house had hit a peak. The wife wanted him gone. The house he hated so much would remain hers, and he did not seem to like that as much as one might have expected from how he talked of it before. Eliza tried to calm him, asked him to sit down, but he paced rampant across the living room rug, wrinkling the fabric into furrowed bumps with each step. All at once, with the energy of a balloon popping, he rushed to the bathroom. The door slammed behind him, separating him from Eliza in the living room.

He could not compose himself, even as he glared back at himself in the water-ingressed mirror. "Stupid fucking idiot. You moron." The words flowed suddenly out; it was unclear who exactly he was talking to. His anger condensed into something he could no longer hold in, and he went on. "Can't do anything yourself, can you? You have to get someone else to fill your holes and you can't even be discreet about it! Making a scene in–this ugly house and everything in it!" Turning with momentum, he kicked the fragile wall behind him. His heel gouged through the wallpaper, sinking in. He pulled his leg back, and the hole remained, exposing the interior of the house.

"Hollow," he muttered, then turned to leave the bathroom. A loose tile finally popped up and gave way. It slid forward; Dane slid backward. The bathtub was waiting to embrace him as he went down. The faucet, though, was waiting to catch the back of his head. It lacked the same cradle in its shape. Momentum fled the scene, and Dane went still, a rosy red paint peeking from where it had made contact with the faucet. It wasn't a color the house was fond of, and Eliza would surely be horrified once she inevitably came to check the bathroom, especially with the thudding sound his collapse had made.

Everything would be okay, though. The bathtub could be replaced, and Eliza would surely think to do so when she saw the danger it could pose. The tile would need to be redone too, and the hole in the wall plastered over. Maybe she would be inspired by this tragic moment to repaint the entire bathroom, too, possibly a lilac or a powder blue rather than the ghastly red from the body. She could make it feel new again, and the bad memories would go away as easily as switching out the hand towels. The police would come, and Dane would find a new home in the ground. Eliza would take care of this, and she would move on. The house would welcome her renovations.

Cowboys
Danny Young

I woke up early on Sunday with the neighbor's rooster and rushed down the stairs in my pajamas to make it to breakfast. Mama made good bacon, and it was worth scarfing down my share, even if she fussed at me that young ladies don't eat that way. I never cared much when she tried to tell me about being a lady. I let her tie my hair back into two braids for school, and listened as she called me a pretty girl, but I couldn't stand much past that. I picked at my eggs, sticking my tongue out at the runny yolk spilling over my plate. Dex sat on the floor beside me, pawing at my chair until Mama stopped looking and I lowered my dish below the table to let him gobble them up.

Papa glared at me from over his paper, his old wrinkly forehead getting all scrunched up as I tried to read the Sunday funnies and ignored him. He didn't tell on me, he never did, only huffed before looking back down and turning the page.

Mama took my plate and was starting to do the dishes by the time Pau came slinking down the stairs, a cigarette hanging out of the side of his mouth. He scratched at his scruffy beard, and Papa gave him a mean look as he poured himself a mug of coffee. I always wondered what Papa would look like with a beard, but he laughed at me when I asked him to grow one. Mama dusted off her still-clean apron while muttering to herself about the smell of smoke spreading through the house. I grinned wide at my uncle, sitting on my knees in my chair with my hands pressed to the table to lean towards him.

"Pau, you goin' to work today? Can I come? I can help."

Mama pushed on my shoulder to get me to sit back in my chair, and Dex yelped as my foot landed on his tail. I winced as he ran to Pau's side who gave him a pat on his head, the mutt sneezing at me. Pau let out a long hum, taking a drag from his cigarette before checking the clock on the wall. Papa shook his head still looking at his paper. "Harley, shouldn't you be studying?" He flipped another page, stabbing at his eggs with his fork. I wrinkled my nose at the thought of wasting the day staring at one of Papa's history books. They were always about war and never had any of the good shootouts or bank robberies like the Westerns on television did. Papa never liked them, so Pau always watched them with me, and sometimes, when he'd blow his smoke out into the living room, he looked just like Clint Eastwood.

Pau shrugged at me, already pulling on his boots, "We ain't gonna take all day. It's summer, Charlie. She'll still have months to read all of them books." He pointed up the stairs while reaching for his hat, "Kit, you got five minutes to get dressed, then I'm gone. Hop to it."

I jumped up from my chair and ran to my room as fast as I could, ducking out of the way of the hobby horse peeking through my closet. Its little brown head swiveled back and forth as I rushed to pull on my jeans and boots and grabbed my hat as I left. Mama called after me to stop running but I was already hopping into the passenger seat of Pau's truck before I even realized she'd been speaking.

The drive to Main Street always felt slow. I counted red cars to keep myself busy until Pau told me to think of the numbers instead of saying them.

"Dumb kid. If you keep counting like that, you'll start to forget your letters." He shook his head, fussing with the radio as he waited for his light to turn green.

I gave him a wide grin and laughed, air whistling through the gap in my front teeth. "That ain't how it works, Pau."

Pau squinted at the road like he was thinking hard before he sucked on his cigarette again, letting smoke spill out his open window. "Whatever you say, Kit, you're the brains, not me."

I stared at him a little longer before my mouth twitched, and I started to twiddle my thumbs. "Yeah, it doesn't feel much like it though."

Pau raised one bushy brow, glancing at me before turning into the next street over. "Whatcha mean?"

I let out a short sigh, picking at the edge of my seat, "It's nothin',,' just sometimes I don't like bein' smart." The vinyl gave way under my nails, and I sat on my hands to stop them from fidgeting, "It makes people think I can handle a lot more than I can."

Pau took another drag before parking the car in front of Grant's Supplies. He turned down the volume of the bluegrass song that was playing before laying his hand on my shoulder and looking at me.

"Kit, I'll give you a tip. People are tough on you because life is tougher. Folks just want to make sure you do good out in the real world. That's why even when things seem too hard, the best thing for you to do is to work harder and stay in school."

I didn't meet his eye, instead focusing on the faded kneepads of his blue jeans. "You never went to school."

He gave a long sigh after that, opening the door and dropping his cigarette to stamp it out with his foot. "Point proven. Come on, we don't have all day."

The door to Grant's Supplies had a bell over it that dinged when you walked inside. Everything was made of wood, and every Sunday an elderly man who only spoke in low angry grunts and had his eyes covered by the constant furrow of his brow would come in the store to clean. I ducked past where he was sweeping behind the canned food and peeped at him through a gap in one of the aisles, holding up my fake finger pistol, and aimed for the bridge of his nose. I could practically smell the sheriff's reward of five hundred dollars for bringing this outlaw in, dead or alive.

"Time to meet your maker," I whispered, closing one eye and squinting, just about to fire. He must have heard me though. In the next moment, his head snapped to look at me and his eyes grew as wide as an owl's. With a shout, I ran retreating to the counter at the front of the store where Pau stood with his hat to his chest, leaning into the blushing face of a lady with long sandy blonde hair. I rammed into his leg, sending him sideways a bit with an 'oomph!' but he stood to recover just as quickly as he had stumbled. The counter lady helped him up, laughing, and I stared perplexed by her perfectly manicured nails.

"Oh goodness, are you alright?" She said, leaning across the counter and then looking at me, "Well hello there little lady."

I tilted my head away from her hands to squint up at her, still clinging to Pau's leg. "I'm a cowboy."

Pau gained his footing again, looking a bit lost for words, and stuttered his way through an apology before turning to fuss at me. Before he could get anything out though she waved him off.

"Oh, don't apologize, I know how it is. My niece is just the same." She talked with her hands and Pau began to smile before she carried on, "It's just so nice to see a father hanging out with his kid." The smile slowly dropped from Pau's face, a distant look on his face as he turned to look down at me staring back up at him with big round eyes.

"She ain't my—" he was cut off by Mrs. Grant coming around the corner, her heels clicking on the floor as she huffed.

"Well, would you look what the cat dragged in. Paul, I know you're not flirting with another one of my cashiers."

I peeped up from behind Pau's leg and Mrs. Grant's narrowed brown eyes softened at the sight of me. "Hey, Harley honey, you helpin' Paul today?" She slid a caramel candy over the counter, and I was quick to shove it into my mouth.

"Yes ma'am," I said. Pau heaved a sigh, wrapping an arm around my shoulder.

She nodded to herself before turning to the counter lady. "That's Charlie's girl. Do you know Charlie?"

The counter lady's eyes went wide as she blushed an even deeper red, "Oh, I'm so sorry, I thought she was yours."

Mrs. Grant tapped the counter and shook her head, looking at Pau with a heaving sigh and narrowed eyes. "Yeah, you'd think that huh? You two always seem attached at the hip."

I lit up at the sound of that. People always thought I was Pau's little girl. He said it was because I followed him like a lost kitten, so he called me Kit. I never saw it as a bad thing though. Pau was a good person to follow. He knew plenty about the right way to walk and how to talk himself out of trouble. I learned plenty trailing after him, even if Papa didn't like it too much. After Pau came to live with us, Papa always mumbled about how he hadn't been able to keep himself out of trouble since they were tots.

"Yeah, well she's just good help, that's all. Speaking of, I'm looking for paint. Ms. Carter needs a new coat on her fence." Pau shrugged, and I watched as one of his hands dropped to his back pants pocket, grabbing at his cigarettes before letting it fall again.

Mrs. Grant stopped her tapping and stared him down for a moment. It was a mean look that Pau turned away from, and I tilted my head in wonder of why. It didn't last long as in the next moment she was turning to grab the paint buckets behind her. "White or blue?"

Pau paid for two buckets of white paint, and then we were back in his truck. I counted blue cars this time, including his since there were fewer of them, and Pau said nothing. When I turned to look at him, he was biting his lip and had both his hands kept firm on the steering wheel.

"I think that lady liked you, Pau," I said, and Pau scrunched his face up tight giving a small smile.

"Yeah, maybe so."

I kicked my feet, looking at my boots and the little pink lines painted into the brown leather. "Maybe you could marry her since you don't have a wife yet." I heard Pau scoff, "and maybe then I could come live with you two when you buy a house together."

Pau lit another cigarette, "Marriage ain't that simple Kit, and I can't buy a house."

I felt that he was just being difficult, but didn't go on, instead I watched the cop car that came crawling up beside us at a stoplight. It sat lower than Pau's truck, and the officer driving it turned to glare at us through the window. His nose looked crooked. I turned to Pau, my grin sharp but hesitated to say anything as Pau kept his gaze straight. He pressed himself against his seat, and the muscles on his hairy arms tensed where he was squeezing the steering wheel. His knuckles turned white from how hard he gripped it. I tilted my head a bit, trying to make sense of the funny way Pau's eye twitched.

"Does he know you Pau?" I said, trying my best not to whip around and glare right back at the cop. Pau's cheeks turned a little red, and he moved his head just enough that I couldn't see his eyes.

"Don't stare Kit. A cowboy has to mind the sheriff."

I said nothing, leaning back into my seat just like him until the light turned green and the cop passed by us. As we drove, Ms. Carter's house and her faded fence appeared around the bend. She was sitting on her porch with a pitcher of lemonade when we hopped out of Pau's truck. Pau waltzed up to her front steps and I followed behind him, trying to fit into the boot prints he left in the dirt path. Ms. Carter filled two glasses and nearly let mine overflow as she giggled over every word that tumbled out of Pau's mouth, slapping at his arm. I rolled my eyes as she made some comment on liking men rugged, carrying the paint buckets and brushes toward the fence at the end of her front yard. Pau joined me after I'd already painted four posts and I looked at him with a bit of judgment, "She likes you too."

He shook his head, "She likes anyone who will talk to her." He dipped his paintbrush into the bucket twice before swiping it over the fence. Before I could say anything, he was covering my mouth with his free hand, "I ain't gonna marry her, so don't bring it up."

I almost spit on his hand when he pulled it away, "I wasn't going to say you should." I swiped at another post, giving it a funny face before covering it up, "I just think maybe if you had a wife, she could tell Mrs. Grant to stop looking at you so mean."

He breathed out smoke and leaned back to look up at the sky like Mama did when she was praying, "There ain't a woman in the whole damn world who would make Mrs. Grant stop looking at me like that."

I painted a stripe across three posts, my lips pursed into a thin line. "Why not Pau?"

"Because it ain't about the women. It's just me she doesn't like," he said.

I threw down my brush, kicking at the fence post, "Well that ain't fair." He shook his head at me, and I almost kicked him too before I thought better of it.

"No, Kit, it is." He paid me no mind, dipping his brush again, "We can't control how people think of us. We just gotta learn to accept it."

"Well, I think that's dumb." I stuck out my tongue and picked at the grass below me, throwing it up into the air. Pau never did anything to wrong people. He would go out of his way to mow their yards or paint their fences. Mrs. Grant just didn't know him that well, if she did, she'd see why he deserved her caramel candies too. "You're good Pau, a real cowboy."

He laughed a little, though it sounded strained, and tipped his hat down to cover his eyes. "You're a dumb kid," he said, putting down his brush and wiping some sweat off the back of his neck, "But thanks."

We finished the fence by the time the sun was beginning to set, and Ms. Carter giggled and swatted playfully at Pau's arms for an eternity before she paid him. When we made it back to the truck, Pau rubbed at his shoulder where she had managed to smack him with one of her bangle bracelets.

"You should check for bruises."

He gave me a look but still rolled up his sleeve, "Hush up."

When we made it back home, the earth had turned golden, and I ran through the grass of the front yard before Dex tackled me to the ground, sniffing all along my arms and shirt as I erupted into a fit of laughter. Pau came to lay beside us, his hat placed on his chest. I stared up at the clouds, taking in their sweeping hills that laid out like mountains across our flat horizon like in the movies.

I let out a whistle, something I had been practicing for weeks now, and Pau gave me a hum of agreement, though he didn't smile like usual.

"One day I'm going to head out there, and I'm going to have a ranch, and you can come live on it with me," I said, and Pau sighed, sitting up and leaning back on his hands.

"I have to tell you something, Kit." He said.

I sat up beside him, combing away at some of the grass that had managed to get stuck in my hair.

"What's wrong Pau?"

He had this strange look on his face again, like he was far from me, and unable to draw himself back in. I watched him squint at the sun before he looked at me, the crow's feet by his eyes still showing like he was looking at something bright.

"I have to," he paused, his mouth still hanging open for a moment as he took in the tilt of my head, "I'm heading west. I'm gonna go find one of those big cattle ranches you're always talkin' about."

My eyes got big, and I jumped up to my knees to shake him by the shoulders, "Pau! You have to take me with you." I said, begging with my fingers laced together.

He shook his head softly, putting one of his rough hands on top of mine, "No Kit. You can't come."

I felt a deep pain in my chest, stinging enough that I ripped my hands away to wrap around my middle.

"Why not?" I said, soft and cracking as he gazed down at me. He rubbed at the back of his neck; his eyebrows knitted together.

"It's complicated. You have to stay here, with your ma and pa."

He tried to meet my eyes again, but I was too busy picking grass out of the ground, ruthless in my attack.

"Kit, you won't have a life if you come with me. You stay here, you'll get to go to school, get a nice comfy job, and grow up to be someone you should be." He sounded like Papa, and I never hated Pau more. I tried to plug my ears so he would go away, but he grabbed at my arms.

"No, you can't go. It isn't fair!" I shook my head back and forth, kicking my feet as he just rubbed up and down my arms to calm me down. I wouldn't. I refused to stop my fit even though I knew it wasn't helping. The second he let go of me, I knew in my bones he would disappear, so I just kept yelling until his patience ran thin. "I can help. I can be a cowboy. You can teach me."

"Kit, stop. No one needs me here; your daddy asked me to leave so I'm going." He grabbed me tight and shook me. I went still in his arms, "I'm going kid, it's already been decided."

"I need you," I said, my voice soft and my throat tight. The sun felt like it was burning into me, and I wanted to let it, so I could have an excuse as to why I wanted to shrivel up into Pau's lap and have him hold me. He softened his grip, sighing, and looking down to where Dex lay next to us whining.

"No, you don't." He shook his head.

"But if you leave I can't—"

"I ain't your daddy, Kit." He said with finality, and my heart felt cold and alone, "You have one. He's a good man. Don't you ever say he ain't because I was raised with him, and I'll know you're lying. He's already gotten me out of enough messes to make up a lifetime."

I shook my head again, looking down, "He isn't you, Pau."

Pau let go of me, grabbing his cigarettes from his back pocket and shoving them in my face.

"You see these?" He shoved them closer, and I bit at the inside of my cheek to stop myself from snapping back at him

"You think these are good? Do you think any of the things I do are things I wanna see you do?"

It was a pretty box, the red always peeking out the top of Pau's jeans. He took out one of the cigarettes, almost crushing it in his hand.

"This, this is shit." He threw it down and stood up to crush it under his boot. He looked giant, and unforgiving, like Papa when he had found out I had broken one of his old globes playing sheriff.

My nose started to feel runny, and the tight funny feeling in my throat bubbled up until I could feel myself choking on it. The sight of him made my stomach feel hollow, and I ran away before he could say anything else.

He called after me, but I didn't listen, crashing through the screen door right into Papa's arms. He stood shocked as I cried into his crisp white shirt, hitting his sides. The fabric scratched at my face, and my tears left it stained and ugly, but he didn't push me away, so I stayed.

"Harley, what has gotten into you?" He said it lightly, one of his hands placed softly on my back. It felt awkward, and he didn't hold me closer than he had to. He looked around the room, and I knew it was for Mama. I butted my head against his stomach, and he furrowed his brow as he looked down at me. I glared right back, and he sighed, a tired look pulling at his face that made me want to scream.

"Why don't you go clean yourself up, your mother is making chicken tonight, maybe you could help her?" I detached myself from him before I could start yelling, running up the stairs to hide in my room. I sat huddled up in bed, the quilt Mama had made me drawn around my shoulders until the sun had fully set, and I could see the moon peeking up behind the trees through my window. I opened it to hear the crickets sing and leaned out to feel the warm summer air pass over me. Mama had called me to dinner almost an hour before, but I couldn't bring myself to travel back downstairs. Pau would be there, picking his teeth clean of chicken and grunting his way through Papa's questions. They would fight, and I knew this because they always fought, and I would be stuck in the middle of it, trying to defend Pau from any of the nasty names Papa called him. For the first time, I didn't want to defend him.

As I began to count the stars starting to dot the sky, I heard the muffled shouts echoing from downstairs. There was a clattering of plates, and as I sunk to the floor to press my ear up against my rug, I could hear Papa from below.

"—No work for you here! I've tried Paul, I've always tried to help you, but you haven't made it easy. Now you're filling Harley's head with these delusions—"

I listened to Pau grumble something, the first part hard to make out until he started to get louder.

"-Not a damn charity case Charlie, I don't need it, and don't you bring the kid into this. This ain't her mess."

Their voices both came and went, in and out, growing louder and softer until there was a large clattering of plates, loud enough I could hear a glass break and mama let out a shout. It was quiet for a moment after, the entire house falling still. I listened as a chair shoved back and his footsteps stomped as Pau grumbled out a response. The screen door slammed open and shut, and as the smell of smoke began to travel up through the window, I shut it as quickly as I could. It felt too late though, my eyes were already watering, and as much as I tried to blink them away, stubborn little tears managed to escape me. I called them shit.

I must have stood there for ages, staring out my window and crying, because by the time I came back to myself the moon had risen above the trees. There was a knock at my door, and instead of spitting and cussing every nasty word I knew, I moved to slide down against it and knock back, too tired to do much else.

"Hey, Kit."

"Hi, Pau." I wanted to call him shit. I crossed my arms across my chest and felt as he slumped against the door on the other side to sit beside me.

"Did Papa tell you that you have to leave tonight?" I looked down at the streaks of light from the hallway that wrapped around his shadow and stretched across my floor.

"He warned me about a month ago. He just tried to give me money," he said.

"Oh. Did you take it?"

"No."

"Oh." I wanted to curse him, tell him he was dumb, and have him get angry with me so I could have an excuse to do so. I couldn't bring myself to.

"I'm sorry I didn't tell you I was leaving sooner," he paused for a moment, I heard his head rest against the door with a small thud, "I didn't know how to tell you."

My chest felt tight, and I pulled down my hat to cover my eyes. I didn't say anything, not trusting my voice. The door's white paint was chipped at the bottom, and I picked at it until Pau knocked again.

"You still there, kid?"

I brought my knees to my chest, hugged them tightly, and closed my eyes shut.

"I could be a good cowboy Pau," I sounded so shaky and small, like Dex when Mama yelled at him for doing something bad, "I am one."

Pau didn't say anything back for a while, but I could hear him bump his head again, and I wondered if he felt as small as I did. "I know you are, Kit. You're better than me," he said, speaking softly but the crackly sound in his throat still broke up his words so he sounded like one of Papa's scratched records. I never wanted to sound like that. "You have to give these things time, though. One day when you're older, you'll still be walking around in your boots, and you'll be better than all of us at whatever you decide to do with your life." I could hear the smile in his voice as he spoke, and fighting against every angry bone in my body, I opened the door.

He had to tilt his head up a little to look me in the eyes from where he was still sat on the ground. It was like he was just seeing something for the first time. His eyes were a little watery, and they squinted up at me like I was a stranger, but there must have been something he recognized because he grinned wide, and I was pulled down into his arms.

I let him tug me down and rested my head against his chest to hear his heartbeat. It thundered like the sound of horses.

"You're a good man, Pau. Mama and Papa are lying." I said.

He nodded his head and rocked me in his lap. It wasn't easy as I was getting taller and my legs stuck out a bit too much to be comfortable, but his arms still cradled around me like I was precious.

"You are too, Kit."

After he gathered all his things from his room and shoved them into little boxes and bags, I walked him outside. I carried his duffle bag across the yard, and he pretended not to notice as I struggled a bit to get down the front steps. By the time I made it to his car, he had already thrown everything else inside. He took the last bag and threw it in his front seat, dusting off his hands after. I copied him, pretending not to hear him snort.

"Guess this is it, huh kid?"

I looked up to where he stood, hands on his hips and his head facing towards the open road.

"Yeah, for now. I'll see you again though." I said, shrugging and wiping my still runny nose.

"That so?"

"Yeah, when I get a car, I'll drive out west until I find you."

He looked down at me, his eyes going all soft, "Not gonna give up on me?"

I shook my head, grinning up at him, "Nah, you need someone looking out for you."

He gave a big whooping laugh, his head shooting back. I laughed with him, so hard that I had to brace my hands on my thighs to keep myself from falling forwards. Pau pulled himself together after a while, sliding into his front seat with a hopeful spark in his eye.

"I'll send you a postcard once I find somewhere to settle down, then maybe, when you get that car, you won't have to just wander around for too long." He said, fiddling with the radio until bluegrass began to belt out of his truck.

"Okay Pau, don't forget."

He tipped his hat to me as the truck started up.

"I won't."

He drove away after that, and I held my hand up to reach for his car until he disappeared down the street, the light from his headlights fading into the night sky above.

A Promise From You is a Fickle Thing
Savanna Peveto-Kreatschman

I felt the sweat drip down my back as I moved the clothes across the wooden washboard. The humidity made it feel like I was moving through the hottest, thickest fog imaginable. I continued my to-and-fro as the sun beat down on my back. I had been at this for so long that my hands were sure to be stuck in that position, which was only going to make it more difficult to do again tomorrow. Even after years, one never got used to this sort of discomfort. I shouldn't even have to do this; I'm no peasant.

Time dragged on as Sól made her way home, leaving us in the cold embrace of Mani, her unforgiving half. I looked up to the sky as if they had the advice I craved. As if they themselves could make mischief settle for the mundane.

I looked up, watching as the last rays of light fled the sky. How did this become my life? I got up, hung up the dripping clothes as quickly as possible so I could get inside before the creatures of the night awoke. I have had enough of them for my lifetime...... and yet.

—

Looking up, I admired the sun dancing through the leaves of the Evergreen Ash tree. What a beautiful beast, towering over the world and all the creatures that roam it. As I gazed on, the anxiety and anger I felt slowly melted away. I felt an emotion that I couldn't explain, a sort of wholeness that I had never felt before. I closed my eyes, feeling the breeze graze my skin. I don't know how much time passed before I felt the gentle kisses against my neck, right above the collar of my linen night tunic. I kept my eyes screwed shut, afraid that the slightest breach of the outside would cause the smooth lips against my skin to vanish.

"You left."

The lips paused for a second before resuming their sweet assault on my skin.

"I've missed you," I breathed out. "It feels as if every minute is itself a year. At first, I thought you had been called away on business, but by the third winter month, I realized you weren't coming back," I hesitated, "You left us."

The lips disappeared and I knew that when I opened my eyes, I would be greeted by the clay walls of the prison I had been abandoned to, the home I never wanted. So, instead of allowing reality back in, I lay there in the grass under the tree, the yellow of my eyelids the only thing I saw.

—

That was the first time He visited me in my sleep. He never spoke to me, but I felt His presence, his feather-light kisses, his long hair drifting over my forehead as He held me. Now I wake up, only to go through the motion in anticipation for the sun to disappear, to close my eyes and find myself in his embrace. Some days were harder than others, today was one of those days.

The rain was non-stop, thunder shaking the Earth. Despite the weather, today was still meant to be a celebration. The men of the village were returning from a battle, all the young women gathered at the shore to welcome them home... all except me. All men had been ruined for me; I could never be satisfied by someone other than him. So, instead of enjoying the festivities, I had shut myself away, listening to the faint echoes of a cacophony of cheers and joy. I did this to myself, my father liked to remind me. I was fair and youthful, with long white hair and a pale complexion. I was blessed by the Gods, marked with their favor, and could have any man I wanted, but I refused. He was the only one I would have, even if *He* would not have me. I know I was, but I pawn in His game, but I enjoyed every blissful second.

Finally, the sun was down, and I could sleep. I had been waiting all day, as had become my routine. My parents would not be back until near sunrise, only to spend the following day sleeping off their spirits.

I closed my eyes, waiting to feel the sun on my skin. I waited one minute.... Two minutes...... Three hours? I held still, not moving a single muscle, waiting for the change. It never came. Giving up, I slowly opened my eyes, only to be greeted by the murky gray light filtering through the cracks in my roof.

I had hoped this was an isolated event, but as each night passed, I became more and more weary. Something was wrong. Sure, he left often, but this was different. I could feel the emptiness in my soul. It was as if he disappeared from the face of the earth. Maybe he had. What if he had been taken? I had to find out what had happened. But how? I got up, pacing to help myself think. It's not like I could go ask the gods. That would be like asking for death. No, I needed someone to act as a medium, someone above us mere mortals, but more reasonable than the gods. I needed a seer, a priestess of sorts. I needed to see the völva. However, in my village we had none. I would have to travel to one of the neighboring villages, about a two-day journey from home.

I started packing my bags, doing my best to stay quiet as my parents had returned already. I needed to leave before they awoke. I knew that they would try and stop me. I knew that, while my dad respected and honored my lover, he did not approve of our intimacy, though he would never admit it out loud. However, he, as a mere mortal, did not have the power to do anything about it.

I left as quickly as I could. It was dull outside, the sky above a mixture of shades of gray. There was a slight drizzling of rain, but no breeze. All I could feel was the thick humidity, soaking my skin and slicking down my back beneath my tunic. The air was heavy and oppressive. It was going to be a long journey.

I had made up my mind. I would find him. Whatever it takes. He would never leave me like this, leave our unborn child like this, unless something was very wrong. After leaving the town, I swiftly followed the path in the woods. I was hoping to make this trip as short as possible, but that was not an easy task. The path was small, barely large enough for one person; hardened dirt worn down from many travelers, but difficult to find in the underbrush now as it was no longer used. That was due to the creatures that had slowly taken over the forest as the villages had become less nomadic and more domestic. The warriors had stopped hunting the monsters and now they ran rampant. Instead of fighting the forest creatures, our warriors instead fought each other. There was never peace between all of the villages. Someone always wanted what someone else had.

I made my way farther through the forest, brambles catching on the thin wool sleeves of my dress. I felt the thorns scraping against my skin. Every time a leaf crunched under my shoe, I stopped where I stood, anxiously holding my breath as if at any moment a forest creature would burst through the underbrush, ready to rip out my throat. I continued on this way until sunset. I was more afraid of the creatures lurking in the dark than the ones that inhabited the day, so with a sigh of contentment, I found a nearby tree fit for me to climb. I got as high as I could, which was only about 7 feet in the air, as the higher up I went, the smaller the branches became. It was there that I got settled for what was sure to be an incredibly long night.

—

It was. I did not fall asleep easily and when I finally did, I could not stay asleep. Between the fear of what creatures could be capable of climbing trees might be skulking around, as well as the completely rational fear of falling to my death. Gods, wouldn't that be a way to go? I could already hear the village wives' gossip:

"Brave enough to travel the forest, dumb enough to fall from a tree."

"What a foolish girl thinking she could hold the attention of a God."

I scoffed, reminding myself that soon those women wouldn't matter. Once I found him, I wouldn't have to go back. The rest of my life would be full of peace and luxury, not having to worry about the opinions of those cruel women. He had Promised. And anyways, those women acted like they cared, but all they cared about was whatever interesting things were going on with others to distract themselves from their own bland and depressing lives.

It felt like an eternity as I watched the sun slowly creep above the horizon. As soon as it became just light enough to fully see my surroundings, I made my way down from the tree. I couldn't waste any of the daylight. I hadn't even reached the small village between mine and the one in which the priestess I had heard of resided. As I walked, the path got a little wider and clearer. I sped up as I started to see structures through the trees.

I approached the hill at the edge of the small clearing where the village was. It was a lot smaller than I had expected; I could see the entire village from my vantage point. I decided to stop at the village to gather some supplies, and hopefully find a place to rest for the night, as I wouldn't make it much longer in my condition.

I dragged my feet down the path and into the village. The few people around stopped what they were doing and stared at me. I could imagine what I looked like; my once neatly tied up hair had started coming loose, falling down in thick strands. My long, previously white dress was littered with small holes and stains, the bottom stained brown from dragging along the dirt. I knew my face couldn't be much better from all that I had been through. The journey to the next village, the one I was actually heading to, would be much easier as the wood thinned out the further North you traveled. After a minute or two of wandering the town, someone finally approached the crazed, hag-like woman I must have appeared to be.

"Are you well, dear?" the woman asked kindly.

"Oh, umm, yes. I'm looking for a place to stay the night," I said quietly.

"Oh, you are poor dear. There's no Inns here. You see, we don't get many visitors in our little village." Seeing the disappointment on my face, she quickly backtracked, "Of course, I have plenty of room in my house. Really. It's been awfully lonely since my husband passed; I would be grateful for the company." She smiled, the sincerity shining in her eyes.

"If it's not a bother," I replied hesitantly.

"Oh, of course not, dear. I would love to have you stay the night. In fact, I accidentally made too many fish, so I'll be glad to have someone help make sure none of it goes to waste."

With that reassurance, I followed the kind woman toward the middle of the village, where her home was located. There the lady gave me a tour of the small structure, as well as fed me the most delicious fish that I had ever tasted. I couldn't believe how lucky I was to find such a generous and welcoming woman. After dinner, she showed me to a guest room, one she explained was usually for when her sister came to visit her. She also showed me to her bathroom, where I was able to shower before settling down. The house was smaller than my, but more homely and warm than I ever knew possible. The bed was soft, the covers warm and thick. It didn't take long for me to drift to sleep.

Something was pulling my hair. My mind was filled with fog, still halfway asleep. I didn't want to get up yet. *Another tug*. My eyes shot open. Something was very wrong. I sat up quickly, spinning around shuffling away from the sight before me; the kind woman from last night was crouched on all fours, thick strands of my hair hanging out of her mouth.

"Hush now dear, there's nothing to be afraid of," She spoke in a quiet, gravelly voice, once again reaching for my hair. I scooted farther back out of pure shock.

"O c'mon deary.... Chosen by the God's.... Delivered straight to me... You are my gift! I was once just like you; A pretty young girl who captured the attention of a God. But I was barren. He left me, forgot me. At least that's what I had thought. But here you are. With your white hair, practically a big bow with my name on it if you ask me. And don't forget that blessed womb."

I couldn't believe what was happening. I mean, I heard of things like this happening. Women going crazy after being left by a God. Thinking they were special, only to be cast aside for whatever sparkling object caught the God's eye next. It was pitiful. Imagine wasting your life away all because you were obsessed with something you couldn't have.... It was just sad.

"My sweet child has finally been brought to me," she screeched, reaching for my stomach.

"NO!" I finally broke out of my shock induced haze. I scrambled backwards off the bed, rushing towards the door, swinging it open, and stumbling quickly out of the dark house.

"YOU CAN'T TAKE MY BABY! MY BABY! MINE! IT'S MINE...." I could hear her broken screams echoing well after I made it through the village and onto the path through the thinned woods. I ran until I could no longer, collapsing on the ground, trying to restart my heart. My heart slowed. My breathing deepened. I was so tired....

—

You will find me; of that I have no doubt.

—

The sun had disappeared behind the clouds, the cool wind pushing through my knotted hair. I would need to redo it before I reached the village, but my scalped ached from the chunk that wicked woman pulled out. I will never forget the look in her eyes, like she was begging me to recognize her, to see her. She was pathetic.

—

It hadn't taken more than a few hours to make it to the village where the priestess was located. The sun had barely reached its peak at the center of the sky, however, still faint as the clouds started growing thicker and darker in the sky. It was most likely going to rain. I was so relieved to finally have reached the village, everything would be over soon.

I adjusted my hair one last time and made my way into the village. I wasn't sure how to find the priestess, but I assumed that I would come across it if I just kept walking. This village was much larger than the last, as well as the one I grew up in. Eventually, I found it. It wasn't hard to see when I got closer. It was a small dark building with large runes carved into the wood wherever there was room. Pots, bowls, and all sorts of other containers were scattered across the ground surrounding the building. A fabric curtain hung in the place of a door, rich with colors even though it looked as if it had been worn down over decades. I hesitantly approached the entrance, pushing the fabric aside. I shivered. It was freezing, so unlike the world right outside the small building.

I'm not sure what exactly I expected, but it was not what I saw. The inside was very different from the outside. It was a simple table with two chairs, one with the back to the door and the other on the opposite side. The room was bathed in warm candlelight, perfectly illuminating a young, beautiful woman sitting at the table. Behind her, a countertop cluttered with herbs, utensils, and a large basin. There was a small hallway in the corner, leading to a bedroom, presumably.

She was extremely tall, even sitting down she was taller than me, even though I was considered above average height for a woman. Her hair was dark black, as if you were staring into the darkest night, almost grazing the ground. She had a heart-shaped, perfectly proportioned face. Her dark eyes were trained on me as I slowly entered.

"Is there something I can do for you?" the woman asked with a thick, gravelly accent. I had traveled so far for this; I wasn't going to let some giant women scare me.

"Yes, I am looking for someone."

"Ah, I see. Whom do you belong to?"

"*I'm looking for someone. I am my own,*" I replied sharply.

"And I can tell exactly who it is," she replied indifferently. She motioned for me to sit down and began to explain the situation to me.

—

Three nights...She said she would find him. I would come to her house each night, starting tonight, and by the third night she would know where he was. Why had he left? I thought she would judge me, or at least think I was crazy, but she acted as if this was a normal occurrence for her. But it didn't matter. Nothing did, not when I would be with him in just three days.

—

I left my room in the inn that Dagrún had directed me to. She had explained how the process tonight would go: we would sit and meditate, and after she would read her runes. I didn't understand how that would do anything, but she was the priestess, not me.

I walked from the inn to her house, the whole time thinking about how it would feel to be with him again. I wondered if he would look different after all this time... It wouldn't matter, I would recognize him no matter what. I couldn't wait to be in his arms again. To feel safe for the first time since before he disappeared. He was all I needed in this world. Baby or not, if I had him, I would be happy.

—

I wish I could say that the meeting was like nothing I had ever experienced; something more amazing and awe-inspiring than I could have imagined.... But I can't, and it wasn't. That might have been the single most boring couple of hours in my entire life. All I did was sit there as she prayed. And meditated. And prayed again. Or at least I think she was praying. She had her eyes closed for so long that she very well could have been sleeping. I wish I had been sleeping.

The worst part of it all was that she became angry at me everytime *I* had to use the restroom, or when *my* stomach growled. The next day I knew I would have to make sure to eat before making my way to her house. I wouldn't want to offend "the great priestess." It's ridiculous really. Before the baby, I was never hungry like this. I'm practically ravenous. *It* constantly needs something. I miss living for myself. But it doesn't really matter, not now. Not when I'm so close. Not when *we* are so close.

—

After two extremely long nights, it was finally time. I woke up, immediately hopping out of bed. I could not possibly be more excited than I was. I was going to be with him. I just had to pass the time until that night.... Impossible. I sat in my room. Stood up. Walked around my small room. Sat back down. Picked up a book. Opened it. Put it back down. I needed to get out of that small, suffocating room.

115

I left the inn, walking to the village market I had noticed when walking to Dagrún's house. I walked around, listening to the idle chat of the villagers.

"Oh, yes, my mother has been feeling much better!" A young woman selling her wares was telling a customer. I continued to listen to their conversation, starting to really be interested. That was before I heard something alarming from behind me.

"—saw him early this morning... he looked very mysterious."

"Oh, do tell me what he looked like!"

I quickly looked over my shoulder, seeing two young girls, both dark haired and tall, following at a distance behind their mother. I walked a little closer as they stopped at a stall.

"He is the most handsome man I have ever seen," the slightly taller girl gushed. "He was so tall. I didn't get a chance to see his eyes, but I saw he had long blonde hair and looked so strong. I just know he could throw me round." The girls giggled to each other and continued their conversation, but I couldn't focus. I knew it was him. I had no way to prove it, but I knew. He was here for me. I couldn't breathe. I ran to Dagrún's home to tell her. It worked! He was here! I stumbled, my dress getting wrapped around my legs, but I didn't care. All I care about is him.

I threw open the door gasping for breath. I looked up, staring straight into the eyes of Dagrún.... Except it wasn't Dagrún, not really. The eyes were the same, but her face was almost... *distorted*. The features, well, everything except for the eyes, were wrong. I didn't really understand what I was looking at. It seemed like her, but also not. I couldn't tell what about her appearance was off exactly, but I just *knew* it was. I slowly took a step forward, away from the door.

"You're here early," Dagrún replied enthusiastically.

"I— yes, I am."

"Well, is there something I can help you with? We can't start until tonight, if that's why you're here." *It* turned away, rummaging through herb-filled containers littered all over her cabinet tops.

"No, no. That's not it. I heard something today, I heard—" I stop, my eyes zeroing in on the back of *his* head.

"Well come on now, what was it that you heard?"

I said nothing.

My vision tunneled until all I could see was that. One. Blonde. Streak.

I felt my blood heating underneath my skin, and *not even the Gods would be safe from my fire.*

Creative Non-Fiction

The Execution of Lady Jane Grey
Grace Harmon

Of all the paintings in London's National Gallery, my sister was most captivated by this one.

At first glance, I couldn't see why—the portrait was a rather tragic one, depicting a seventeen-year-old Jane Grey reaching for the chopping block, blindfolded, moments before she was decapitated in order to secure the British throne for Mary Tudor. She had only been Queen of England for nine days.

As I looked closer, I began to see what had drawn my sister in. The raw emotion in Jane's face, the sense of helplessness, and the weight of her tragic fate all seemed to speak to something deeper. It was something that resonated with her in a way I hadn't initially understood. Many tourists had simply scanned the piece and snapped a photo before walking away. Others would even pose for a photo in front of the massive portrait, smiling with their hands placed awkwardly at their sides, before scurrying away to locate the other reputable gems the gallery had to offer.

Katie stood motionless, her legs crossed and hands resting on the leather straps of her backpack. She seemed to be an island amidst the ebb and flow of onlookers, who moved around her as if she were the one obstructing their path. From my vantage point behind her, I could only see the back of her head, but it was clear she was deep in thought, absorbed by the painting in front of her despite the steady hum of tourists murmuring as they passed by. When I approached her, I asked why she circled back to this particular painting in a building packed with Monet's and Van Gogh's.

At first, Katie simply told me that the painting was much bigger than she had imagined. In truth, it was enormous, nearly consuming the entire wall with its staggering 8 x 10-foot presence. Perhaps it was the sheer scale that made it so overwhelming—there was so much to absorb. The details were striking: the devastation etched on the faces of Jane's handmaidens, one of whom pressed her head against the cold stone wall, while the other gazed into the distance, seemingly avoiding the harsh reality of their mistress's impending fate. Then there was the man guiding the blindfolded Jane, his hand firm yet tender as he led her toward the execution block. Even the executioner, standing just beyond, seemed caught in a moment of hesitation, the axe resting idly at his side, his bright red leggings stark against the grim scene unfolding before them. The depth of emotion in each figure felt almost tangible, as if the painting itself was alive with the weight of their suffering.

From our position in the gallery, it was simple to gather that not one person in that room wanted Jane Grey dead. Each person in Paul Delaroche's scene sympathized for her in their own unique way. Her death only served a single purpose—to pave the way for Mary Tudor to claim the British throne.

Katie and I stood there for a while, taking in the last few moments of this young girl's life. I remember thinking how strange it is, to be transported back to such a pivotal moment in British history by the mere method of pigments and oils. I had spent all day roaming the halls of the National Gallery, looking at priceless art crafted by some of Western culture's most renowned artists, featuring depictions of heaven and hell, of cities I would never travel to, of people I would never see or read about, but none of them quite captured me like Jane Grey did.

We left the gallery shortly afterwards, perhaps feeling a little over-superior to the world, in the way that truly seeing the "art" in art can make one feel.

Later that same day, Katie and I found ourselves wearily climbing the stairs from the tube station. We made our way back to our hotel off St. Katharine's Way, following our usual route that wound past the Tower of London. It was just after the sun had set, at the point in the day where the last bit of blue clung to the sky, offering a thin veil of light before the streetlamps finally flickered on.

Katie and I skipped down the slanted street that made our thighs burn as we climbed up it that same morning. She pointed to our right, to the Tower of London just across the street, and reminded me about Jane Grey. Our hotel was just a block away from the tower, and we had passed it many times before. I had even stopped to take pictures of the magnificent, albeit intimidating piece of architecture prior. The moat was now filled with orange poppies, swaying delicately in the breeze to commemorate all the death that happened across the centuries on this one plot of land.

On that day, I looked at that 1000-year-old castle resting on the Thames River, and thought of how, within a span of nine days, the Tower of London went from being Jane Grey's castle to her prison. Nothing in this world is entirely predictable—that which we find power in can just as easily become our ruination. But Jane never really had any power. She was a figurehead for one of the most powerful empires in the world but couldn't wield any of it. Although her nine-day reign ended very differently than it began, she consistently held the same amount of power, nonetheless. She merely occupied the British throne the same way a pawn occupies a square on a chess board.

She simply held space.

Mexican American Daughter
Erika Valiente

Growing up a Mexican American, not speaking fluent Spanish was not a problem. I could understand. I could pass with a few words. Plus, I was surrounded by American culture. There was no need for Spanish. At least that was my mindset until I hit sixteen. The age of my raging adolescence. During this stage of my life, I do not remember the many times my father has seen me cry, but I remember how his bare hands made me feel. The way his calluses and sandpaper hands held my emotions. By placing both palms on my tear-stained cheeks and forcing me to swallow his words with my eyes, my father said to me, "Es tu mamá." She is your mom. "Aunque no la quieres, ella sigue siendo tu mamá." *Although you may not want her, she continues to be your mom.* "Habla con ella." *Talk to her.*

My mother and I had been at the stage of constant disagreement. I could not express my feelings in her language. She could not express her feelings in my language. So instead, we talked through the language of silence. But my father did not understand this, so I stared at him. I wanted to believe him. I wanted to believe his hopes for a mother and daughter to reconcile. But his views seemed far different from my experiences. "Ella no es mi mamá." *She is not my mom*, I said. "No lo entiendes. No puedo hablar con ella" *You do not understand. I cannot talk to her.* I felt alienated. I felt angry. Angry at the silence that dominated my mother and me. I wanted to ask her, "Did I do something wrong? Did I hurt you?" I wanted to ask her if our language was the cause of our separation. But she was unknown to me, so I never did.

At seventeen, it had become so natural for my mother and I to not speak that I forgot the day we stopped having conversations. Maybe we started when I lost my accent. I would talk, but my pronunciation would speak first, ruining the attempt to tell her about an event at school. And I would try again. This time I would prepare the words and sound out the syllables under my breath. But gradually as my voice became smaller from each mistake, my words would too. The words I once knew would become nonexistent until eventually they became the language I stopped speaking.

Since then, I have never told my mother about anything in my life. And as an adolescent, I thought this was fine. I did not need to speak to my mother. I had my American friends. I did not need Spanish. But as I grew older, my longing for her did too. I would watch her talk to my older sister who knew Spanish. I would watch them converse and wish to join. I would watch her cook and wish to join. When we looked at each other, I would wish for her to smile at me. When we were alone, I would wish for her to turn to me and say, "Lo siento. Empecemos de nuevo." *I am sorry. Let us try again.* As I grew older, I began to share the same hope as my father. The hope for my mother and I to reconcile. But the inevitable barrier built between our chests allowed no chance for communication.

Because of this, being a teenager was not easy. I did not have my mother guide me into womanhood, which made discovering my identity harder. I did not have my mother to talk about my conflicting emotions. I was lost with no direction. I became angry and transformed into another person. It was a surprise for her. But more of a surprise for me, the day my emotions collapsed.

She had picked me up from school and as soon as I entered the car, I glared at my mother and said, "¿Me odias?" *Do you hate me*? When I did not hear a response, I asked her again louder. "¿Me odias?" As I looked at her, I realized the one resemblance we shared—her almond-shaped eyes, which slowly softened when she finally said,

"No te odio." *I do not hate you.*

I was swarming with the anger of not verbally being able to express my feelings that I began screaming at my mother, "Tu me odias!" I cried. *You do hate me*! At this point, I was uncontrollable. I felt the years, the months, and the days aching for my mother gush out of my body. I felt the urge to know why she stopped caring for her daughter.

"¿Por qué me odias? ¿Qué te hice?" *Why do you hate me? What did I do to you?*

My anger became sadness. And yet, with tears blurring my eyes, I did not see her turn my way throughout the ride—not once. My mother did not reply to me throughout the ride—not once. Instead, the silence between us became my cries throughout the ride.

A year later, now eighteen, the slightest hint of summer had begun to shed. Days before my high school graduation, I asked her to dye my hair. Reluctantly, she agreed and started spreading the strong aroma of the formula onto my scalp. Like my father, I could feel her calluses and sandpaper palms as she repositioned my head with each touch. With her hand methodically painting each strand of hair, I felt her concentration. My mother had never touched my hair as mothers did to their daughters. But maybe, she simply was not like other mothers. Maybe she simply was not like other mothers who expressed their love physically. When she finished, I turned to her and said,

"Gracias, mami." *Thank you, mom.*

She looked away and whispered, "Ve a bañarte, Erika." *Go take a shower, Erika.*

Through this, I slowly began to understand the way she loved. While on our way to browse graduation dresses, "Lento" by Julieta Venegas began to play on the radio. My favorite song. Once I started singing, my mother looked at me and said, "¿Te lo sabes? A mi también me gusta este." *You know it? I also like this one.* She reached for the radio, turned the volume up, and as the chorus was coming, together we sang, "Sé, delicado y espera. Dame tiempo para darte, todo lo que tengo." *Be gentle and wait. Give me time to give you all that I have.*

When she came back from a garage sale one Sunday, she quickly ushered me to her room filled with an array of clothes. "Mira este. Lo elegí para ti." *Look at this one, I chose it for you.* The scene reminded me of the time I got my finger stuck inside a jewelry box. I was the age of my youngest sister when mindlessly I began wandering away from my mother at a local garage sale.

Presumably overfilled with child temptation, I reached my finger inside the old box when suddenly, like a Venus flytrap, it closed. Through my roaring cries, my mother found me, gave me a mint, held my hand, and brought us home. It was memories such as these that revealed her invisible acts of love. So, I grabbed the orange flannel with the *Betty Boop* design, knowing I would never wear it, and said,

"Gracias, mami." *Thank you, mom.*

A few days later, I graduated. After my family's festive mood was over, I quietly celebrated myself by replenishing in the warmth of June's sun. During these times of solitude, I would wonder if perhaps I had been born in Mexico, would my mother and I's relationship be different. I would also wonder if the relationship with my relatives would be different too. My graduation party consisted of my mother's side of the family. Aunts, uncles, and cousins from different areas of the country came together to celebrate my commencement. They would say, "Felicidades! Te deseo lo mejor." *Congratulations! I wish you the best.* I would reply with a simple thank you as I could not express anything more. However, others would begin asking deep questions that needed sentences as an answer. "¿Cómo te sientes ahora una muchacha? *How do you feel now as a woman?* "¿Que estudiaras?" *What will you study?* This time, I would reply with a simple laugh and say, "No sé." *I do not know.*

I have felt the same countless times in the presence of my language. That summer was the first time I caught a serious cold in a while. And since my family's health insurance was no longer available to us, I was reluctantly brought to a doctor connected to some Mexican locals. The ladies there were nice. One of the nurses was way too beautiful. The way her Virgencita necklace curved with the way of her pronounced collarbone. The way her accent naturally mixed with the softness of her voice. Her long, straight hair with just a simple pull-back style exposing the frame of her Latin features. God, she was everything I wished to be. A true Latin woman.

My mother asked her, "¿Y de dónde eres?" *Where are you from?* She gently smiled and replied, "Soy de Cuba." *I am from Cuba.* This attracted my mother's attention and at once she began conversing with the nurse. As I watched them, I noticed the liveliness in her expressions. My mother did not have many Latin friends. Nor did she have many family members in the United States. The ones she had only came for special occasions. Suddenly, the nurse turned my way and asked, "¿Y por qué estás aquí hoy?" *Why are you here today?* Before I could even talk, my mother took matters into her own hands and responded for me. She told her my symptoms. She told her about my allergies. As my mother spoke, I simply listened and watched.

Once we sat in the car, I looked at her and said, "Era bonita." *She was pretty.*

My mother nodded her head, "Para la próxima, pagarás." *Next time, you are paying.*

I laughed, "Ya lo se. Gracias, mami." *I already know. Thank you, mom.*

The Stand-In
Mae Bradley

I'm surrounded by colorful blocks and children's books that pull me back in time to age 5 when my dad still lived at home and read me bedtime stories. The sterile smell of cleaning agents tickles my nose as I lean my head back to rest on the warm window of the Children's Museum in Downtown Lake Charles. The hum of a projector in the room, neighboring my little library, permeates the heavy silence spilling into the hallway. I shut my eyes to pretend, even if only for a moment, that the world is not yet lonely, and that I am not yet turning 19.

Only two years ago, I sat in this same spot while living a completely different life. It was before I got the news that changed everything. The day after my last visit to the museum, I sat in my living room with my mom. She rambled on behind me as she braided my hair, telling me how glad she was that I chose to grow it back out for graduation. I did my best to hide my misery, knowing that after the ceremony I'd be able to cut it all off again. My phone felt heavy in my hand, and I glanced at it over and over, waiting for a phone call from my dad. My mom tugged the half-done braid on the back of my head each time she felt me pull away to look down. Despite her frustration, I couldn't help but to whip the braid from her clutches at the feeling of a vibration in my hand. It was a text.

The clacking of plastic hitting plastic coaxes my eyes open as Eddie stumbles into the museum library over green, red, and blue legos as big as the palm of my hand. A block castle, built carefully by the kids who played here before I seized the room for myself, sits to the left of the doorway. Stepping over a landslide of toys, Eddie places a hand firmly on its roof to balance himself. The structure creaks beneath his weight before crumbling to the ground. I'm startled by the resulting sound but not shocked to see the destruction.

After a moment, Eddie stumbles to sit beside me, doing his best to avoid stepping on any green army men. He drapes one arm over my shoulder to pull me into him and leans his back against a cold slab of brick wall in lieu of the glass pane behind me. The thud of his heart beating behind the fragile skin of his chest brings me comfort for a moment. A raspy whisper escapes his lips as he holds my head firmly with one large, slender hand. "Happy Birthday."

I mumble an acknowledgment and burrow further into him, caring more that I'm not alone than about anything else.

Today is no different than the day I got that text. It was Eddie showing up for me that day, too. Forgetting my mom's annoyance, I read through the message in front of me. Eddie and I had only been on a couple of dates, but he had no problem being there for me. Sometimes he could even be a little too there for me. He texted me to inform me that he was coming to my house with ice cream. I relayed the information to my mom, and she let out a much louder sigh than any of the ones produced by the moving of my head moments before. Before I could respond, the quacking duck ringtone—that signified my dad calling—rang out loudly and I brought my phone up to my ear almost as quickly as I pressed "accept call".

Today, the sickly-sweet smell of maple syrup from Eddie's recent shift at Waffle House fills the air around me. I try not to choke. We stay there for a while, maybe out of comfort, or maybe because I know that trying to move away might present an opportunity for him to struggle against me. Several minutes pass as I go elsewhere in my mind, allowing my surroundings to fill my senses and send me into a memory of resting my head on my dad's shoulder while home sick from school in the 6th grade. I threw up on him that day. That same nauseous feeling creeps over me as I return to the present, and I fling myself back to escape what suddenly felt more like a chokehold than a hug. My eyes focus on a blue leather folder that rests inconspicuously on the plastic coffee table that only held books when I last checked. Eddie smiles a big, crooked smile and carefully picks up the folder, presenting it to me without a word. I lift the cover and the smell of freshly printed ink on paper wafts into my face, almost suffocating me with unexpected potency. I try not to cough. Blurry text on a single page reads "Star Certificate: This document certifies that a star has been named in honor of Coraline." I stifle a scoff of displeasure. He knows I hate it when he calls me that.

Eddie was always bad at knowing what to say or do for me. When he showed up at my house two years before, I was already crying. My dad thought a phone call to be the perfect delivery for the worst news possible. "Hey, Tiny," his voice felt like a hug around me even as he was hundreds of miles away. I couldn't quiet my voice as I happily announced the date of my graduation to him. I paused for a moment before quietly asking, "Do you think your work trip will be over by then?" I heard a labored sigh from the other side of the phone. "The work trip has been over for a little while now. I'm staying in New Orleans with Jessie's family. We've been house hunting." I immediately forgot about the details of my graduation and began screaming with tears dripping off my chin. My mom must have heard enough to understand what was going on. She took the phone out of my hands and tagged me out, beginning to berate and yell at my dad with anger I hadn't seen from her since he left me the first time. I stood up to follow her as she walked into her room with my phone, but I couldn't make myself take a step until I heard a knock at my front door. When I opened it, Eddie stood in front of me with a shopping bag containing my least favorite flavor of ice cream. I would have reminded him how much I hate coffee, but his arms were around me before I could get a word out. I shrieked in his arms and his shirt became saturated where my head rested on his chest. He kept holding onto me even as I tried to pull away, crying out that my dad left me for his other family.

Now when I glance back up at Eddie's face, his expression is blank, as if he's searching for some sort of hint about what's happening in my mind. I plaster a big, half-hearted grin across my cheeks and give him a hug. As long as he can't tell how I really feel about his idea of a gift, I'll be fine. He holds me in his arms for just a little too long, only allowing me to break free when my phone begins to vibrate.

I slide my finger across the screen to accept the call and hear my mom's voice on the line as I raise my cellphone to my ear. Her timing couldn't have been better. I fake a frown and tell Eddie that my mom is waiting for me downstairs. He insists on walking me down to meet her, stopping our progress on multiple occasions to request a kiss. Each time, I oblige, hoping that each would be the last. Every thud of his feet in the stairwell rings in my ears like the ticking of a clock, counting down to the next moment where he might make a demand for more. After what feels like an eternity, we're standing at the front door.

With one final peck on the lips, Eddie and I part ways. As I place the leather-bound certificate in the passenger seat of my mom's car, I look back at the building one more time. I can see the remains of the piled-high legos in the third story window. The smiling sunshine logo above the doorway glares at me, as if to urge me forward. The moment I clip my seatbelt in place, my phone vibrates again in my pocket. The screen glows brightly with the word "DAD" on glorious display. I answer quickly with a giant, painful smile.

"Hey, I wanted to give you a call to let you know we just finished moving into the new house," he says, before I could even squeeze out a greeting. I pause with expectation but quickly realize that's really all this is about. "I hope you'll change your mind and come visit sometime soon," he continues after a prolonged moment of silence. After that, the only sound is the quiet whine of country music on my mom's radio for what seems like minutes. I fight to choke down hurt words, but eventually they slip out.

"I'm 19 today."

"Oh. Well, happy birthday," my dad says in a voice meant to disguise his surprise. I recognize his tone and my heart sinks into my stomach. I thank him in an attempt to sound polite and end the call abruptly before he can hear the quiet tremble in my breathing as tears roll down my cheeks.

My thumb hovers over the screen of my phone, moving into position over the messaging shortcut Eddie set up for me when we first started seeing each other. His contact appears immediately when I press it, and I type out a short message between the teardrops falling across my keyboard.

"Hey, are you free tomorrow?"

Silence of the Lambs
Jarely Rebollar

These words are echoes from an old diary, pages inked by a young hand struggling to understand, to name, to trust. I was barely twelve, caught between the weight of what I was taught and the whisper of something different, something dangerous. These lines hold my search for grace, my hope that love was not beyond God's reach.

I

Growing up, love was spoken in whispers, like secrets slipped through the slats of confession, promises passed in shadows. I learned early that love, the kind I felt, was a threat. Love was not the simple kind, not the kind that rested softly like a wafer on the tongue. It was jagged, sharp enough to pierce, and I had to hide it away, a shard of myself kept between me and the God I hoped would understand.

Nights were the hardest. Silence swallowed the words that felt too large for my mouth—words like her and I love. In the dim light of a candle-lit altar, I searched for a prayer to make me whole. But the more I searched, the more I unraveled. Maybe whole was just another word for holy. Maybe love was a language only silence could speak.

II

There was a day when I stood before the cross, looking up, and I wondered—if He could stretch His arms wide enough for the world, could He stretch them wide enough for me? Could He hold a heart that refused to follow, a heart that broke its own rhythm, danced its own beat?

And maybe, yes, maybe love isn't a sin. Maybe love is the way we find holiness in the fractures. Maybe, in my own quiet way, I've been praying all along. Every whispered I love you, every silent night I stitched myself together, became my own psalm, rising like incense in the hush of darkened rooms.

III

There's grace here, I think, a grace born not from permission but from knowing, from seeing that holiness is never flawless.

Holiness is a cracked vessel, a light cast best through broken glass. And maybe now, as I look at the open arms of the crucifix, I see not a judge but a witness to my truth, a reminder that real love— the kind that survives silence, survives shame, survives fear—is the deepest prayer.

It's enough, I think, to hold my head high, to feel the pulse of this faith that loves me as I am. Here, in this soft, trembling acceptance,

I am whole.

Scholarly Essays

Food Insecurity
Kayla McKinley

In 2019, the United States' Department of Agriculture found that 13.6% of American families were experiencing food insecurity and this is only expected to get worse because of inflation (Daundasekara, et al.). Economic difficulties, increased by the struggles that accumulated during the COVID-19 pandemic, are causing an uptick in food insecurity. The effect of food insecurity often manifests itself through malnutrition and bad health. This can affect growing children and older adults with a ripple effect that only continues to decrease their quality of life. However, this is not the fate that must be accepted as a reality without any hope of intervention or change. The truth of food insecurity has inspired many individuals and groups to foster community gardens and food banks to provide a way for others to get the much-needed fuel for their bodies to stay as healthy and happy as possible.

COVID-19 brought about many changes in the world, but one impact it had was to help increase the number of individuals who are now facing food insecurity due to financial difficulties. According to statistics, "In 2018, approximately 11.1% of U.S. households experienced food insecurity [1], yet a recent analysis... found that rates of food insecurity have doubled overall and tripled among households since the COVID-19 pandemic began" (Poulos, et al.). COVID-19 impacted everyone's lives. Some lost jobs, some lost family members, and some started to experience another kind of pain—hunger. When people struggle financially, they tend to find it hard to afford the most basic need: food.

Economic difficulties not only accentuate the hunger many families face, but also provide a leading cause of not having the resources to buy food. As Daphne C. Hernandez reports in her research article, "cumulative financial strain was related to experiencing marginal food security over food security among non-poor households" (Daundasekara, et al.). As pointed out in the following statistic, poverty is naturally associated with food insecurity: "In 2021, 32.1% of US households with an annual income below the federal poverty line were food insecure" (Suhood, et al.). For financially strained individuals, expenses other than food and groceries prioritize how and what they spend (Suhood, et al.). This hardens the viciousness of financial turmoil and pain of food insecurity because people have to choose between necessities such as housing or food (Suhood, et al.).

Sadly, the main impact that food insecurity creates is malnutrition, which leads to bad health. Food is essential to quality of life. As noted by the American Institute for Cancer Research, eating the right food can prevent 40% of documented cancer (Suhood, et. Al.). Growing children especially need food in order to meet the minimal amount of energy and nutrition required for threshold growth and health rates. One article, which talks about health status that children experiencing food insecurity may have, states that the children often are, "more likely to report poor general health, experience chronic health conditions, including asthma, eczema or other skin allergies, depressive symptoms and poorer mental health, and acute health conditions such as cold and stomach problems compared with peers in food-secure households" (Daundasekara, et al.). Older adults are also at risk for nutritional deficiencies according to another article, "Seniors who are food insecure have lower average nutritional intakes by between 8% and 24% for eleven different key nutrients...the burden of current and worsening chronic health conditions that accompany food insecurity can lower self-reported physical health" (Suhood, et al.).

Awareness about food insecurity has caused food banks and community gardens to spring into action. In addition to providing nutritious food, community gardens encourage people of all ages to live healthy lifestyles and to engage and invest in their local communities (Suhood et al.). One of the biggest issues with community gardens is that individuals do not have the time or money needed to maintain the garden (Suhood et al.). When this occurs, the garden can fall into disuse and disrepair. Food banks partnering with healthcare providers have also experienced difficulties on several fronts (Poulos, et al.). Among other problems, lack of good leadership, communication, data sharing and food insecurity knowledge contribute to a disarray of what was intended to be beneficial to the community (Poulos et al.).

Difficulties surrounding these food bank and healthcare partnerships include misconceptions that healthcare providers may have about food offered by food banks, as stated in an article, "inability of food banks to ensure consistent food products or produce at any given time of the year...their ability to purchase food largely depends on funding and the ability to safely pack, transport, and store foods [23]. As noted by results, healthcare systems may have unrealistic expectations of what food banks are able to deliver" (Poulos et al.). Food banks and community gardens do their best to help despite the continuous difficulties they face as they provide resources to their communities.

Economic difficulties, increased by the struggles that accumulated during the COVID-19 pandemic, are increasing the difficulties that already food insecure-families and individuals face. The effects of malnutrition and bad health can adversely affect growing children and older adults by decreasing their quality of life. At the moment, there are many challenges facing organizations seeking to implement solutions. In order for a beneficial change to occur, all individuals in every community must take the initiative to end the tumultuous hunger that has plagued our communities. As food banks, community gardens, and other charitable efforts try to decrease the harmful impacts and stop the causes of food insecurity, they will need the general public's help. These organizations and programs rely heavily on volunteers and donations to continue to support their communities. While many efforts are being made to promote progress on the issue of hunger and food insecurity, challenges remain steadfast as many seek to eliminate food insecurity.

Works Cited

Sarah Suhood, MS, BS; Chayanne Robinson, BS; Carmel N. Tovar, BS; Sydney E. Love, BS; Bridgette Kielhack, BS. "Public Health Practice Commentary Community Gardens: A Tool for Public Housing Complexes to Combat Food Insecurity in the Older Adult Population." TPHA Journal, Volume 76, Issue 2 pp. 8-11.

Natalie S. Poulos, Eileen K. Nehme, Molly M. O'Neil and Dorothy J. Mandell. "Implementing food bank and healthcare partnerships: a pilot study of perspectives from charitable food systems in Texas." BMC Public Health, 2021, pp. 1-7.

Sajeevika Saumali Daundasekara, Brittany R. Schuler, Daphne C. Hernandez. "A latent class analysis to identify socio-economic and health risk profiles among mothers of young children predicting longitudinal risk of food insecurity." PLOS ONE, August 24, 2022, pp. 1-23.

Guy Montag's Transformation in *Fahrenheit 451*: A Fight for Freedom

Mohamed Irhabi

In *Fahrenheit 451*, Ray Bradbury presents a dystopian world where books are banned and firemen ignite rather than extinguish fires. The story centers on Guy Montag, a fireman whose transformation from a loyal enforcer of society's anti-book laws into a seeker of knowledge and truth serves as a critique of censorship. Montag shows the will of an individual against the oppression wrought by society. Throughout the novel, Montag develops into an extensive and psychologically transformed individual with a rising awareness of opposition toward a civilization that restricts the freedom of the intellect.

At the beginning of the novel, Montag is portrayed as a "minstrel man, burnt-crooked" (Bradbury 2), a fireman who takes pride in his work of burning books. His encounter with Clarisse McClellan marks the first step in his transformation, as she asks him, "Are you happy?" (Bradbury 7). This question upsets Montag's confidence and confronts him with the void in his life. Clarisse's curiosity and willingness to question the status quo leaves a lasting impact on Montag, causing him to start questioning the purpose of his work and the society in which he lives. Her disappearance only makes him more anxious over how this suppression of individual thought has taken place and how censorship has been used as a means of maintaining order in society.

Montag's doubts grow stronger when he witnesses the suicide of a woman who chooses to die with her books. This act provokes a deep feeling of guilt and irritation in Montag, who finally realizes that there must be something in books worth dying for. He cannot resist the urge to know "what the books say," as Captain Beatty phrases it (Bradbury 59), and grows progressively uncomfortable with his society's superficiality, including his wife's addiction to mindless entertainment (Television and movies). This internal conflict is evident when, one night, Montag hides a book under his pillow. Beatty's explanation that limiting choices prevents people from becoming politically unhappy, "If you don't want a man unhappy politically, don't give him two sides to a question to worry him; give him one" (Bradbury 58), where he exposes the government's strategy of keeping people compliant by eliminating complexity and dissent.

The transformation of Montag accelerates when he meets Faber, a retired English professor. Faber helps Montag by guiding him in the pursuit of truth. They create a plan together wherein the firemen will be challenged by printing books and planting them in firemen's homes. Faber gives Montag an earpiece called a "bullet," through which they can hear each other. Even though Montag is determined, he finds it hard to let go of the propaganda he's believed in for so long. This becomes clear when he suddenly reads a poem to Mildred and her friends, leading to an emotional reaction. The scene shows how society fears books because they bring out strong emotions. One of the women says, "Poetry and tears, poetry and suicide and crying and awful feelings" (Bradbury 97). Montag's choice to read out loud, even though it goes against the rules, shows he is becoming more frustrated with censorship and is ready to risk everything to find the truth.

In the final quarter of the book, Montag's change is complete when he escapes the city after killing Captain Beatty. This act shows he has fully broken away from his old life, choosing to be an outcast and a fugitive. He runs to the river, which carries him away from the Mechanical Hound and the censored city, symbolizing a cleansing from his past life. When he meets Granger and the other "book people," Montag finds a new purpose in their mission to save literature by memorizing books. His knowledge of the Book of Ecclesiastes gives him an important role in the group, showing how he has gone from being someone who enforced censorship to someone who protects knowledge. The city's destruction in the war offers a chance for a new beginning, as Montag and his new friends hope to rebuild a society that values intellectual freedom.

The novel is set in a dystopian world where technology and government control individuality and limit intellectual growth. The author, Bradbury, uses Montag's transformation to show the dangers of censorship and stress the importance of thinking freely. Montag's journey from an obedient fireman to a rebellious seeker of truth shows how determination can help someone overcome inner conflict and pressure from society. Through his challenges, Montag learns to accept uncertainty and reach for a deeper understanding of life.

In conclusion, *Fahrenheit 451* shows the human ability to change and the power to stand up against oppressive systems. Bradbury's novel is a warning about the dangers of censorship and a reminder that the fight for the freedom to think is an ongoing battle in today's world.

Works Cited

Bradbury, Ray. Fahrenheit 451. 1953. New York, Simon & Schuster Paperbacks, 19 Oct. 1953, jghsenglish.edublogs.org/ files/2015/02/Fahrenheit-451.pdf.

In Sickness and Undeath
Paxton Holmes

Vampires, bloodsucking supernatural beings have become quite the staple in horror media. Perhaps for their supernatural charms or possibly because of their monstrous qualities, they have been portrayed in many different ways throughout time. One of the more popular and well-known portrayals of vampires is the story of *Dracula* written by Bram Stoker and published in 1897. A story told through journal entries and letters that follows the main characters and their struggles against Dracula, a vampire from Transylvania who can turn other people into vampires. As one of the most well-known vampire stories and just one of the most famous vampires in media, this story has been analyzed time and time again in many different ways. There have been many questions and speculations over the text and why Bram Stoker wrote what he wrote. One of these questions is what drew him to write a story about vampires. He was very sick as a young child and dealt with a lot of bloodletting so this may be what drew him to write about bloodsucking creatures. Through the lens of the psychological term, repetition compulsion, it is possible to understand how these traumas might have influenced him. To understand how this could be an explanation as to what drew Bram Stoker to vampires, an understanding of the key elements involved is needed to fully support this statement, starting with his illness.

Abraham "Bram" Stoker was born November 8, 1847 in Clontarf, County Dublin, Ireland to Abraham Stoker Sr. and Charlotte Thornley Stoker. He was incredibly sick as a young child, and it was believed that he was sick and completely bedridden until the age of seven. The actual illness itself was never officially known, thus, there are no known records of what he had. A fact that is possibly reflected in the story of *Dracula* as when Lucy Westenra first falls ill the other characters are unaware of what she has. It isn't until Dr. Van Helsing arrives and reveals that Lucy is suffering from the effects of vampirism. Due to this, it is possible that Bram Stoker used his own experience with the mysterious nature of his illness to create a sense of mystery and horror in the story of *Dracula*.

Continuing with his experiences with his illness, he was subjected to many treatments throughout his young life, one such treatment being the process of bloodletting. Bloodletting was a common practice, although it began to decline in the 18th and 19th Centuries which is when more modern medicine practices were becoming more common. The process of bloodletting itself was the removal of blood from the body to, in theory, rid the body of any disease or unwanted conditions. This was often done through several methods although the three more common methods were through the use of leeches, cupping, or simply taking a sharp cutting element and cutting the skin. Blood removed using a cutting element was often taken from the neck or the forearm however if a tool such as a fleam was used it would most likely be taken from a vein in an elbow or forearm. Leeches were small segmented worms with round mouths that held multiple sets of small sharp teeth. These teeth allowed them to attach to their hosts which they do to suck the blood out of their hosts. Bram Stoker's experience with this medical practice very likely could have inspired him or drawn him towards the idea of vampires. After all, vampires are known for drawing blood from their victims using their sharp fangs to puncture the skin and drink the blood that comes out.

Bloodsucking creatures and illnesses are often connected both in *Dracula* as well as in the real world. Besides leeches being connected to this idea through their use in bloodletting, another creature commonly associated with this idea would be mosquitos. Mosquitos are small insects that have long, small, needle-like mouths that are used to penetrate the skin and draw blood. These small insects can carry diseases such as malaria, the dengue virus, the yellow fever virus, and many more. When drawing blood, there is a chance they can pass on these diseases if they are infected, causing their victims to fall ill especially if not properly vaccinated. Another such insect commonly associated with the drawing of blood would be fleas. While more commonly associated with animals such as dogs and cats, they will go after humans and can also spread disease and parasites. Diseases and parasites that can be spread include the plague, murine typhus, and tapeworms. In *Dracula*, the role of the bloodsucking creatures is filled by the vampires such as Dracula himself or the three female vampires who go after Jonathan Harker. The "illness" or "disease" is the curse of vampirism that Dracula spreads most notably to Lucy Westenra, turning her and changing her into a vampire. The vampirism is represented as an illness and, as mentioned earlier, isn't fully revealed until Dr. Van Helsing reveals the truth. There are several metaphors for infection throughout the story in both the sense of actual "illnesses" as well as more socially, both of which are discussed in great length in the article *A Parasite For Sore Eyes: Rereading Infection Metaphors In Bram Stoker's "Dracula"* by Ross G. Foreman.

With Bram Stoker's experiences with his illness and with bloodletting, especially at such a young age, an argument can be made that these were rather traumatizing events. Even if they didn't affect him in an incredibly significant way, they still likely affected him since the events happened when he was so young. This brings us to the theory of repetition compulsion. Pierre Janet and Sigmund Freud, French psychologist and Austrian neurologist, both had found a connection to their patients' traumas and to what they did. In similar manners, they found that many of the traumas their patients had experienced motivated them, even after large swaths of time. This need to seek out these traumas is generally referred to as "repetition compulsion", although it is good to note that there still aren't many studies on this topic despite the fact it is referenced and the theory has been around for an ample amount of time. The general theory though, is that people with trauma are subconsciously drawn to things that relate to their traumas, even if the connections aren't always immediate. In many cases, this is represented in more extreme cases such as trauma related to abuse, and the situations in which these people find themselves tend to lead to them experiencing this trauma again. However, an argument could be made that people with not as extreme trauma can still be affected or that the situations they find themselves in can simply be reminiscent of their trauma. This brings us back to Bram Stoker and his experiences. The events he had experienced most likely did have some, even if only a little bit, of an effect on him from a psychological standpoint. Using the theory of repetition compulsion it's possible that he was drawn to the idea of writing about vampires due to his experiences with bloodletting and how vampires drain the blood of their victims. From the view of a child, a person taking their blood and a creature that steals blood from people would possibly be one and the same. Not only that but a creature that infects you and makes you "sick" would be a fear for someone who was very sick as a young child and had some level of trauma from it. It's possible somewhere in Bram Stoker's mind, that there was just enough of a connection from the vampires to his experiences that it's what drew him towards writing a story with them.

But what if it wasn't his own experiences with illness that drew him towards vampires, what if it was the experiences of someone else that drew him towards the idea of vampires? One such person who could have inspired him was Bram Stoker's mother, Charlotte Thornley Stoker, who was believed to have been a fairly influential figure in Bram Stoker's life both as not only his mother but as a storyteller.

Charlotte Thornley Stoker was born June 28, 1818 in Sligo, Ireland. In 1832, an epidemic of cholera spread throughout the town and in many other places throughout Europe such as Germany, France, and England. Mrs. Stoker's own family had made it through the epidemic but not without their trials and not without witnessing many deaths that followed within that time. Many years later, Charlotte Thornley Stoker would write of her experiences and what she had remembered of that time in *Experience of the Cholera in Ireland 1832*. In it, she would go on to describe a rather graphic scene of a man being buried alive and another who almost was. The first was a man who had been sick on the side of the road and then quickly forced into a pit by people who feared the disease. They would then go on to bury the sick man alive, with no empathy to be found. The second account would be an account of an older man who had once been a soldier who had contracted the disease and supposedly died. However, when they went to break the body's legs to fit it in the coffin he awoke and would later go on to recover. These two events very possibly inspired Bram Stoker when it came to writing about the vampires in his story. This is seen as we learn in Dracula that the vampires sleep in coffins with dirt from where they are from, which is why Dracula himself has several boxes filled with this dirt that Dr. Van Helsing must bless and purify so that he can't use it anymore. The idea of these corpse-like people rising from the earth or coffins is very heavily connected between the actual accounts and the story. One would have to imagine that it would be rather unsettling to suddenly see a hand burst from the ground or someone you thought to be dead suddenly awaken, an unsettling feeling that is often heavily associated with vampires and just *Dracula* in general.

As mentioned with the man who was buried alive, the people who did it only did it because they were terrified of the disease. Mrs. Stoker would write more about how bad this fear was as she mentions how they weren't let into towns when her family left Sligo and even wrote how she believed they would have been killed if someone in charge hadn't intervened. People were killed without mercy or empathy, they were killed and buried because they were terrified, and fear makes people do terrible things. Logic went out the window and there was only fear, a feeling that can be applied to *Dracula* as the characters don't know what to expect and most do not have any idea of what they're dealing with. They're not sure who to trust or if they can trust, and people who were once friends and lovers turn into something completely unknown as they're infected, becoming bloodsucking monsters of the night. This uncertainty and uneasiness is very reflective of the time of the epidemic in Ireland which leads to the idea that Bram Stoker was very likely inspired by the event.

One last example that could have inspired Bram Stoker is the part of Charlotte Thornley Stoker's writing where she writes about a man and his wife. The wife had been in pain and so her husband brought her to a hospital where the doctors would later tell the man that she had been sent to the dead house. The man went to find her body to give her a proper burial and found her alive with his red handkerchief. At least this story ended happily as she went back home and recovered. While possibly a bit of a stretch, the couple, in a way, are somewhat reminiscent of Jonathan and Mina Harker in Bram Stoker's *Dracula*. They are reminiscent in a way because the couple goes in both directions. Jonathan falls ill and Mina tends to him helping him recover, later Mina is bitten by Dracula and Jonathan does what he can to try and help where he can so that he can save her from becoming a vampire. In the end, both succeed in keeping the other alive and live their lives together. While a bit of a stretch, one could make the argument that Bram Stoker heard the tale of the couple and wished to replicate such a thing within his own story. A bit of hope in an otherwise dreary and dark world.

Overall, there are many arguments to be made as to why Bram Stoker decided to write about vampires. Perhaps it was for their supernatural charms or simply because he thought they were interesting monsters. But with all the information we have, from his childhood to the writings of his mother, plenty of evidence points to the idea that he was inspired by one of the two if not both. By truly looking at the way vampires are used and portrayed in the writings of Dracula, it is a very good bet that Bram Stoker was inspired and drawn to them due to his own experiences of illness and bloodletting as well as his mother's experience with the epidemic of Cholera in Sligo, Ireland. He used what he knew of the fear of disease and the uncertainty of such things to craft the vampires that he wished to portray, allowing for a deeper narrative experience that allows the characters to grow and reflect the world.

Works Cited

Luebering, J.E.. "Bram Stoker". Encyclopedia Britannica, 4 Nov. 2024, https://www.britannica.com/biography/Bram-Stoker.

Kuriyama, Shigehisa. "Interpreting the History of Bloodletting." Journal of the History of Medicine and Allied Sciences, vol. 50, no. 1, 1995, pp. 11–46. JSTOR, http://www.jstor.org/stable/24623553.

Bessel A. van der Kolk. "The Compulsion to Repeat the Trauma
Re-enactment, Revictimization, and Masochism"
Psychiatric Clinics of North America, Volume 12, Number 2,
Pages 389-411, June 1989.

Raikar, Sanat Pai. "bloodletting". Encyclopedia Britannica,
11 Oct. 2024, https://www.britannica.com/science/
bloodletting.

Britannica, The Editors of Encyclopaedia. "leech".
Encyclopedia Britannica, 4 Nov. 2024, https://www.
britannica.com/animal/leech.

Forman, Ross G. "A PARASITE FOR SORE EYES: REREADING
INFECTION METAPHORS IN BRAM STOKER'S
'DRACULA.'" Victorian Literature and Culture, vol. 44,
no. 4, 2016, pp. 925–47. JSTOR, http://www.jstor.org/
stable/26347269.

"Mosquito-Borne Diseases." Baylor College of Medicine, www.bcm.
edu/departments/molecular-virology-and-microbiology/
emerging-infections-and-biodefense/mosquitoes.

"About Fleas." Centers for Disease Control and Prevention,
Centers for Disease Control and Prevention, www.cdc.gov/
fleas/about/index.html#:~:text=Fleas%20are%20
small%20insects%20that,plague%2C%20or%20cat%20
scratch%20disease.

"Charlotte Matilda Blake Thornley: Bram Stoker Estate."
Bramstokerestate, www.bramstokerestate.com/
charlotte-matilda-blake-thornley.

Stoker, Charlotte. "Experience of the Cholera in Ireland 1832." The
Green Book: Writings on Irish Gothic, Supernatural and
Fantastic Literature, no. 9, 2017, pp. 11–18. JSTOR, https://
www.jstor.org/stable/48536136.

McGarry, Marion. "Dracula as cholera: The influences of Sligo's
cholera epidemic of 1832 on Bram Stoker's novel
Dracula (1897)." Journal of Medical Humanities, vol. 44,
no. 1, 17 Nov. 2022, pp. 27–41, https://doi.org/10.1007/
s10912-022-09763-0.

The Innate Goodness of Nature:
Transcendentalism in Mary Shelley's *Frankenstein*

Savanna Peveto-Kreatschman

Abstract

This article will discuss the Transcendentalism Movement and its main themes as shown through Mary Shelley's novel *Frankenstein*. First, the history of the movement, the main beliefs, the more well-known writers in the movement influence through this movement are acknowledged in order to better understand the movement and its effect on literature. There are three main themes of the Transcendentalism Movement shown through this novel. The first is the importance of relationships. Relationships are a key theme in the novel, as it is often what helps Victor remove himself from his obsession and fear of his creation, the creature. The second theme is trusting one's intuition. Often throughout *Frankenstein*, Victor must rely on his intuition to make morally correct decisions, as well as when he is attempting to fix his mistakes. The third theme is the effects of nature. Nature is important throughout the novel, not just as symbolism for the power of nature over science, but also for how it is able to revitalize Frankenstein and console him during his worst moments. In the novel, nature represents the goodness that all humans are born with. This is in direct opposition to how science is portrayed: corrupting and unnatural. It is important to also take into account Mary Shelley's history, as well as her personal beliefs, to better understand her writing and the messages she hoped to convey through it. While it is commonly known Mary Shelley's *Frankenstein* was heavily influenced by Romanticism, a movement similar to Transcendentalism, it is also important to note the ways it was influenced by the Transcendentalism Movement.

Key Words: Transcendentalism, Romanticism, Gothic Literature, Industrial Revolution, Individualism, Innate goodness

The Transcendentalism movement in New England was a literary, philosophical, and spiritual movement that started in Concord, Massachusetts, lasting from 1830 to 1855. The movement centered around ideas of the innate goodness of humanity, the importance of trusting one's intuition over logic, and the harmony of nature. It was the center of a generational dispute dividing the older generations from the younger. The movement began with pushback against industrial progress, Unitarianism, and the newfound sciences. Those belonging to the movement believed that these things only caused damage to society, and that instead they needed to return to the organic world to let nature heal them. This movement led to the American Renaissance in literature. The movement gained a substantial amount of attention from many well-known authors, such as Ralph Waldo Emerson, Henry David Thoreau, and many more. These authors laid the structure on which *Frankenstein: Or the Modern Prometheus* was written.

The author of *Frankenstein* was Mary Wollstonecraft Shelley, an English novelist from London, England. She did not have direct ties to the movement, however, some of her writing shared similar philosophical and scientific ideas. She emphasized the importance of intuition, unity in nature, and relationships—both family and otherwise. These were all common ideas found in the Transcendentalism movement. Shelley did not, as described by David Hogsette in his article, "write extensively or explicitly about her theological positions" (Hoggsette 8). Meaning that, while Shelley both mentioned God and drew biblical allusions with her novel, it could be inferred that she presented more as agnostic. Shelley was encouraged in her writing by her husband Percy Shelley, despite her works directly challenging his own ideas in his writings. In fact, it was due to a game between Mary, Percy, and their friends Lord Byron and John Polidor that Frankenstein was written. During a stay at the mansion Lord Byron had rented, he proposed a challenge; they would each write a "ghost story." While the story was written as a gothic horror for entertainment, it contains many ideas that were popular during that time.

When researching for this project, I mainly gathered sources that analyzed the religious, spiritualistic, and scientific aspects of Mary Shelley's *Frankenstein*. While these sources do not cover transcendentalism, they discuss common aspects of the movement. One of my chosen sources, *The Life and Letters of Mary Wollstonecraft Shelley*, Volume 2 was written by Julian Marshall, examines Mary Shelley's history and personal letters. This allows a connection to be made between Mary Shelley's personal beliefs and how they affected her writing. While none of my sources share my argument, they aid in providing evidence of the symbolism and underlying messages conveyed throughout the novel.

Corruption of Morals Through Science

Many critics have analyzed the role of science in Mary Shelley's *Frankenstein*. For example, Alexis Hollingsworth asserts the effect that science has on Victor Frankenstein and his morals throughout the novel. Hollingsworth analyzes Mary Shelley's history and personal beliefs as a way to provide evidence for her claims. Mary Shelley believed, as many did during her time, that modern science had been evolving more than should be morally correct, as the actions taken in "the name of science" appeared wrong, as well as against nature and humanity. Hollingsworth discusses the role of the creature and the immorality of its creation. While Hollingsworth analyzed Mary Shelley's personal beliefs and the effect it had on her writing in *Frankenstein*, she did not take into account the Transcendentalist movement and the effect it had on Mary Shelley and her writing.

The History and beliefs of Mary Shelley

While it is important to analyze the novel itself it is also necessary to understand the life and personal beliefs of the author Julian Marshall does this and in their article *The Life & Letters of Mary Wollstonecraft Shelley*. Not only does Marshall provide excerpts from both Mary's personal letters and journal entries, but they also analyze them and how the beliefs of Mary Shelley were portrayed through them; they go on to analyze how these beliefs influence the writing of *Frankenstein*. The author also looks at Shelley's interactions with her step siblings and parents, Mary Wollstonecraft and William Godwin. Marshall goes on to discuss Mary Shelley's relationship with Percy Shelley, her husband, and how they continuously supported each other through their lifetimes.

The Creature's Role in *Frankenstein*

Throughout *Frankenstein* the Creature plays an important role in both the themes of the novel and when portraying the themes of transcendentalism. In Noelle Webster's article, *Mary Shelley's Frankenstein: The Creature's Attempt at Humanization*, she analyzes the ways the novel attempted to humanize the Creature in *Frankenstein*, while also preventing the Creature from being treated as such. Webster starts by discussing who Victor Frankenstein is, as well as the Creature, and their roles in the novel. He also explains Victor's feelings about the Creature and its creation. The author then goes on to analyze the creation of the Creature and the Creature's interaction with the humans he encounters, as well as how these interactions change the way we, as the viewers, see the Creature. By analyzing the Creature, Webster draws attention to the ideas of nature and relationships in the novel.

Nature plays a tremendous part in *Frankenstein*. Throughout the novel, Shelley uses the themes of nature to further the identity of the main character Victor, as well as to highlight the main themes, also held by Transcendentalism, in the book. These themes are: Innate goodness, the healing properties of nature, and nature's signs.

Innate goodness refers to the Transcendentalist belief that all humans are born inherently good, and it is natural for them to do good, and they only become evil due to corruption. An example of this is the creation of the Creature. In the time immediately after his creation, he wishes to do good. An example of this is given by Noelle Webster, who states, "the creature saves a young girl from drowning... The creature's first instinct here is to immediately save the young girl. That shows benevolence in him" (Webster 16). Despite not understanding much about himself or the world around him, the Creature still has a natural desire to be good. When the Creature is conversing with Victor, he says, "'All men hate the wretched; how, then, must I be hated, who am miserable beyond all living things! Yet you, my creator, detest me and spurn me, thy creature...'" (Shelley 71). The creature, still learning, is unable to understand why the man that created him has such a strong hatred for him. This is supported by Kim Hammond in her article, *Monsters of Modernity: Frankenstein and modern Environmentalism*, where she explains that the Creature, "is not a monster because he is somehow 'unnatural'; rather he becomes monstrous first because when he emerges...from the laboratory Victor views him as such..." (Hammond 13). The Creature is still learning about the world around him, and himself, and is looking for guidance. However, due to the neglect of his creator and the mistreatment from society, he becomes corrupt in his morals, killing as a way to take revenge on those who have wronged him.

Another theme when analyzing nature in *Frankenstein* is Nature's ability to heal. There are many instances of this, the clearest being when Victor is returning home. He had previously fallen dangerously ill due to his obsession with his science. When his father sent for him, he was obliged but decided to take a more scenic route home. His travel had a healing effect on him. In the novel, Victor states, "I remained two days at Lausanne, in this painful state of mind...but they were days of comparative happiness, and I think of them with pleasure. My country, my beloved country!" (Shelley 51). Being in nature allowed him to rejuvenate his countenance and regain his strength after being in bad health for so long. Victor is not the only one who experiences nature in this way, In the novel, the Creature states, "'My spirits were elevated by the enchanting appearance of nature; the past was blotted from my memory, the present was tranquil...'" (Shelley 84). By having both the protagonist and the antagonist be healed by nature, Mary Shelley is able to truly stress this theme's importance. It also highlights nature's abilities, as it is able to heal even in the worst circumstances.

A third example of naturalistic themes is the portrayal of nature's ability to send signs. This is shown at the beginning of the novel. As Victor first stumbled on the forms of science that would lead to the catalyst of his destruction, nature sent an event as a way to warn him of the dangers of what he would attempt. Victor acknowledges this in the text, saying, "I beheld a stream of fire from an old and beautiful oak…I at once gave up my former occupations… and entertained the greatest disdain for a would-be science…" (Shelley 24-25). This lighting strike displayed to Victor the raw strength of nature and its capabilities. It was at this time that Victor realized that nature was too powerful for man to overcome. It is further discussed that if Victor had kept this belief, he would have prevented his gruesome future and the deaths of those he held dearest.

Relationships are a prominent theme in both the novel and Transcendentalism. Victor understands the importance of relationships and works hard in maintaining them most. Despite this, his relationships ultimately lead to his downfall. While away at college, Victor became withdrawn from his family. As explained by CSABU in their article, *The Importance of Family in Frankenstein,* "This eventually led to his downfall as the project that he was so consumed in ended up killing most of the people he loved, both directly and indirectly. This may have been Mary Shelly's way of warning the reader that it is important to allocate time for family before it is too late" (CSABU 1). If Victor had, instead, focused on his family and relationships, he would not have created the Creature, therefore causing his own death, as well as the deaths of all his family. While it is important to look at Victor's lack of relationships in certain parts of the novel, it is also important to look at the relationships he does have. Victor's four most important relationships in the text are his relationships with William, Henry, Elizabeth, and the creature.

Victor's relationship with his little brother William, while short lived, provides important insight into his relationships with the rest of his family. Victor, on his way home after the death of William, says, "My journey was very melancholy… for I longed to console and sympathize with my loved and sorrowing friends…" (Shelley 51). After this devastating loss, Victor's first instinct is to connect and grieve with his family. During this he is able to provide relief from the toll that his scientific experiment has taken on him. It also acts as the beginning, foreshadowing the loss and heartbreak that is to come.

The second of these important relationships is Victor's relationship with his dear friend Henry Clerval. Victor and Henry had an incredibly strong relationship. Throughout the novel, Henry is the one Victor turns to, and Henry is always there for him. When Henry came to visit him, Victor had fallen deeply ill. In the text, Victor states, "During all that time Henry was my only nurse… He knew that I could not have a more kind and attentive nurse than himself..." (Shelley 41). This further portrays the depth of their connection, as well as justifies the fact that Victor wants nothing more than to protect Henry from his creation, which is the reason he is unwilling to share what he has done. He hopes that by keeping this information from Henry, as well as the rest of his family, they will be safe. However misguided this may be, it shows how deeply he cares for his loved ones as he chooses to bear the burden of danger on his own.

The third relationship is that between Victor and Elizabeth. They were raised together as cousins, although not blood related, they loved each other passionately. The extent of this is shown near the end of the novel. When Victor rushes into the scene immediately after Elizabeth was killed by the creature, he exclaims, "Why am I here to relate the best hope and the purest creature on earth... Elizabeth, my love, my wife, so lately living, so dear, so worthy." (Shelly 150). Elizabeth represented the only good left in Victor's life, as everyone else he loved had been taken from him by the creature. Elizabeth's death signified the end of Victor, as once she was gone, he stopped living for anything but revenge on the Creature who had stolen so much from him.

The relationship between Victor and the Creature was undoubtedly the most important as it was what drove Victor in his actions throughout the text. In the beginning of the novel, Victor was obsessed with the idea of his creation. He felt both pride and excitement at the idea of creating life, of which he would take a parental role in. However, once he came out of his obsession-induced haze, he saw his creation as an abomination and immediately regretted his actions. He fled from the Creature in fear, therefore abandoning it to the harsh outside world and leaving it defenseless. This effect was only worsened when The creature attempted to befriend a small family, the de Laceys. As explained by Noah Heringman in his article, *Science and Human Abnormality in Mary Shelley's Frankenstein*, "This spectacular reversal culminates in the Creature's transformation into a 'wild beast' when he is rejected by the de Laceys" (Herrington 11). It was at this point in the novel that the Creature realized his efforts to be seen as human would not succeed, and therefore gave up his attempts. When addressing Victor, the Creature says, "How dare you sport thus with life? Do your duty towards me and I will do mine towards you and the rest of mankind" (Shelley 71). Despite the Creature's lack of time alive, he understands the relationship he desires to have with Victor, however, Victor refuses to allow himself to take on this role as a guidance figure for something he deems so sacrilegious. This ties in with the Transcendentalist belief in the abnormality of progressing science, and its transgressions against the natural order.

Transcendentalism is a movement that focuses on the importance of nature and maintaining the natural order of the world. Due to this, they are against the progression of sciences deemed unnatural. This was mainly due to the popularity and influence of the Industrial Revolution during this time, the corruption that was believed to follow this progression of science, the role of morality and the blasphemy of playing God, as well as how science inevitably led to Victor's demise.

The danger of progressing science was not only what drove the novel, but it was also a main theme of Transcendentalism. In the novel, the messages relayed through science are consistent and clear. First, it is important to understand how science came to have a role in Transcendentalism. Once the history on this topic is evident, it is easier to see the influence of science, as well as the transcendentalist themes pertaining to it. These themes are how science corrupts, morality and the effect of playing God, and how science inevitably led to Victor's demise.

The first Industrial Revolution was marked by an era of scientific and technological advancement. It had the biggest amount of influence from the 1800s to 1900s. Not only was this the same time as the Transcendentalism movement gaining popularity, but it was also the time that *Frankenstein* was written. During this time, many were wary of the unnatural possibilities that these sciences could bring, only furthering the strength of the movement. The impact of these fears is evident throughout the novel and the themes directly relating to science.

One of these themes being the ability of science to corrupt. Science was progressing quickly this time. Many did not understand science and were therefore afraid of what it was capable of. This theme is shown best when Victor is in the process of creating the Creature. Alexis Hollingsworth states in her article, *Morality Without God in Mary Shelley' Frankenstein*, "Victor Frankenstein does create a life. He uses the ideas of scientific enlightenment and goes against what was perceived at the time to be morally correct..." (Hollingsworth 2). Many people, especially Transcendentalists, feared this science. Shelley further highlights this as, during the process of creation, Victor falls into an obsessive fit of delirium, fully induced by the dark sciences he was trying to use without fully understanding. In the text, Victor states, "Every night I was oppressed by a slow fever, and I became nervous to a most painful degree... I shunned my fellow creatures as if I had been guilty of a crime." (Shelley 37) Victor was aware that he was acting against nature by creating the Creature, but Science had corrupted him to the point that he felt as if he had no choice but to continue what he had started, despite the physical and emotional toll it was taking on him.

A second theme pertaining to science is that of the dangers of playing God using science, and the effect that had on Victor's morals. He was creating life, going against the Transcendentalist theme that humans were not meant to create nor end life. When thinking on what he had done by creating the Creature he says, "No mortal could support the horror of that countenance" (Shelley 39). At this point, he realizes that, as a mere mortal, he should not have attempted to create life himself. He now understands that this role is not meant for humans, however, he has recognized this too late. This is further supported by Mary Shelley's own words, organized by Julian Marshall in her article *The Life & Letters of Mary Wollstonecraft Shelley*. In one of Mary Shelley's personal journal entries she states, "for supremely frightful would be the effect of any human endeavor to mock the stupendous mechanism of the Creator of the world" (Marshall 74). Shelley firmly believed that humans were not meant to wield the power of creation, which is why Victor's experiment failed so miserably.

The third theme is the role that science, especially when considering the two previous themes, played in the downfall of Victor. Throughout the novel, Victor often feels guilty when recalling that all his loss was caused by his own actions. He states in the novel, "I had been the author of unalterable evils, and I lived in daily fear lest the monster whom I had created should perpetuate some new wickedness" (Shelley 65). This foreshadows the loss of the only loved ones he has left. Due to his creation, he lives in constant fear. After losing everyone he loves, he devotes the rest of his miserable life to killing his creation, as he recognizes that his situation is his fault, and he needs to be the one to fix it.

The Transcendentalism Movement had a significant influence on Mary Shelley's novel Frankenstein. It highlighted themes of nature, the strength found in relationships, and the dangers of attempting a science that isn't fully understood, which were the main messages articulated throughout the novel. This is further supported when looking at the history of the movements occurring during the time the novel was written, and the way they were interconnected. While it is widely agreed that *Frankenstein* is both a form of romantic and gothic literature, it is not as well discussed the way the novel drew parallels to the Transcendentalist movement.

Bibliography

Hammond, Kim. "Monsters of Modernity: Frankenstein and
    Modern Environmentalism." Cultural Geographies,
    vol. 11, no. 2, 2004, pp. 181–98. JSTOR, http://www.
    jstor.org/stable/44250971. Accessed 27 Feb. 2024.

Heringman, Noah. "Science and Human Animality in Mary
    Shelley's Frankenstein." The University of Chicago Press,
    The Wordsworth Circle: Vol 50, No 1, 01 January 2019.
    https://www.journals.uchicago.edu/doi/
    full/10.1086/702587#.

Hogsette, David S. "`Metaphysical Intersections in 'Frankenstein':
    Mary Shelley's Theistic Investigation of Scientific
    Materialism and Transgressive Autonomy." Christianity
    and Literature, vol. 60, no. 4, 2011, pp. 531–59. JSTOR,
    http://www.jstor.org/stable/44314873. Accessed 27 Feb.
    2024.

Hollingsworth, Alexis. "Morality Without God in Mary Shelley's
    Frankenstein." Medium, 8 January 2019, https://medium.
    com/@lexiloulee/morality-without-god-in-mary-shelleys-
    frankenstein-presented-at-swpaca-2017-5c9539466d61.

Marshall, Julian. "The Life and Letters of Mary Wollstonecraft
    Shelley, Volume 2 (of 2)." Project Gutenburg, 8 November
    2011. https://www.gutenberg.org/files/37955/37955-
    h/37955-h.htm#Page_182.

Webster, Noelle. "Mary Shelley's Frankenstein: The Creature's
    Attempt at Humanization." Scholars Archive, University
    at Albany, State University of New York, May 2011, https://
    scholarsarchive.library.albany.edu/cgi/viewcontent.
    cgi?article=1006&context=honorscollege_eng.

"The Importance of Family in Frankenstein." CSABU, 1 November
    2018, https://introtofictionf18.web.unc.edu/2018/11/
    the-importance-of-family-in-frankenstein/.

The Harlot Wears Scarlet: Symbolism in Chaucer's "The Canterbury Tale"

Savanna Peveto-Kreatschman

The Canterbury Tales is a collection of stories written in Middle English. It was written and published between 1387 and 1400 by prominent author Geoffrey Chaucer. The tale covers a pilgrimage to Canterbury, the location of the shrine of Thomas Becket. During the journey, an unusual group of travelers became acquainted and agreed to participate in a game; they would each tell four stories and whoever is voted to have told the best story wins a meal paid for by the others in the group. Throughout the tales written, as not all of the stories were published-whether they were lost or never written is unknown-there are numerous examples of symbolism. The three main forms are: setting, clothing and physiognomy, and character representation.

When looking at symbolism in The Canterbury Tales, it is important to analyze the settings in both the General Prologue and in the Pilgrims tales. Setting often portrays a physical place, a certain time, or a set atmosphere that portrays details about the characters or story itself. In the General Prologue, setting is especially important as it gives context to the story as a whole, as well as sets the tone for the pilgrim's tales.

The general prologue is set in the spring, in which the characters are making a pilgrimage to Canterbury. A pilgrimage is a religious journey to a sacred place, such as Canterbury in this story. However, it is also important to take into account the exact description. In the text it states, "April with its sweet-smelling showers ...when the West Wind also with its sweet breath, in every wood and field has breathed life into the tender new leaves, and the young sun..." (Chaucer 1-7). This description symbolizes renewal of energy, rebirth, and new beginnings. This season, while being accurate as it is the time that people normally went on pilgrimages, was also symbolic of the Pilgrims journey and the inner transformations it would bring about.

Symbolism within the tales of the characters is also important. This symbolism often portrays the main messages in the tales, as well as providing a better understanding of the background and situation set up. There are clear examples of symbolism through setting within the tales told by the pilgrims are in the Nun's Priest's Tale, the Pardoner's Tale, the Wife of Bath's Tale, and the Miller's Tale.

The Nun's Priest's Tale is set in a barnyard. This is a rustic and simplistic setting. The story follows an elderly widow who, as the text describes, "Was once dwelling in a small cottage, beside a grove, standing in a dale" (Chaucer 2822-2823). This plain country setting is symbolic of the disappointing reality of life and furthers the main messages of the table. In this tale there was also a fox's den. This symbolizes deception and danger, themes often categorized as foxes in literature, which were big themes of the story.

Another example where the setting symbolizes something more than is directly stated is in The Pardoner's Tale. The tale is set in a tavern, which is described in the text as a place where, "They dance and play at dice both day and night, and also eat and drink beyond their capacity, through which they do the devil sacrifice within that devil's temple in cursed manner by abominable excess" (Chaucer 467-471). This setting, when you consider that a member of the church was telling the story, symbolizes the temptations of life as well as the moral deterioration that partaking in these temptations can lead to.

A third example of symbolism through setting can be found in the Wife of Bath's tale. While there are multiple settings in the Wife of Bath's tale, one of the most symbolic settings is in the enchanted forest. The text states, "In all this care, near a forest side, where he saw upon a dance go ladies four and twenty, and yet more..." (Chaucer 990-992). This is symbolic, not only of the mysteries surrounding the Old Lady, but also of the themes of magic and paranormal activity throughout the story.

The fourth example is in the Knight's Tale which is set in Athens. It is stated in the text, "He was lord and governor of Athens, And in his time such a conqueror That there was no one greater under the sun. Very many a powerful country had he won..." (Chaucer 861-864). This is a traditional setting for a Knight's tale. It is symbolic of chivalry and order, as this was a powerful city, named after the Goddess of Wisdom, Athena. It is symbolic of the Knight's character, as well as setting the tone for the Knight's story as a classic tale of honor and bravery.

Setting often reveals things about the characters themselves, whether positive or negative. The setting also sets the tone for the story, furthering the messages the pilgrims are attempting to convey. Setting is only one of the main forms of symbolism in The Canterbury Tales. The second type of symbolism is the clothing described in the text.

The clothing of the characters in both the General Prologue as well as the traveler's stories carries a substantial amount of symbolism. Clothing is an important form of symbolism as the outfits define each character and give a glimpse of what lies under the surface. When analyzing this, one can see clear examples in the Prioress, the Knight, the Squire, the Wife of Bath, and the Monk.

The Prioress is described in the text as, "so charitable and so compassionate she would weep, if she saw a mouse caught in a trap, if it were dead or bled" (Chaucer 143-145). This shows her as gentle and honorable. However, this description is in direct contrast with what the symbolism in the clothing worn by the Prioress portrays. She is said to be wearing an expensive cloak, fine jewelry, and a golden brooch. This shows that the prioress cares more for the materialistic, earthly goods than complete devotion to God.

In the tale, the Knight is described as, "a truly perfect, noble knight" (Chaucer 72). He was said to be everything a knight should aspire to be. He was both brave and loyal and was never disrespectful or boastful. His clothing directly reflected this analysis of his character. His clothing, while not poor quality, was not overly extravagant. It was stained with rust, as his armor had seen many battles. While his clothing was not over the top, it was reliable; a perfect representation of his nature.

The Squire was portrayed opposite to how he was meant to be, considering his position as a Knight's assistant. This is shown through his clothing, but not his manner. The tale states, "Courteous he was, humble, and willing to serve" (Chaucer 99). From this description one would expect him to be dressed modestly, with clothes suitable for manual and often dirty work. However, the Squire was dressed in fine dress; a gown with long wide sleeves and embroidered with flowers. This represents the youthful vibrancy and boyish naivete that the Squire portrayed. He did not dress finely with malicious intent, instead, he did this to appear impressive and important.

The Wife of Bath was one of the few female characters and is described differently than any of the other women. Her clothes are rich and fashionable; she wore fresh leather slippers and carried luxurious handkerchiefs. While these pieces of clothing symbolized her expensive tastes, her most important piece is her scarlet red stockings. Scarlet often symbolizes lust and promiscuity. This is validated when it is explained in the text, "She had (married) five husbands at the church door, not counting other company in youth—" (Chaucer 460-461). This was generally not acceptable during this time as any woman with this type of reputation would often be seen as a harlot. They would be shamed publicly, shunned by society, and have very few options in life. Through the Wife of Bath's Tale, the reader can understand how difficult it was for women during this time, as well as see how Chaucer criticizes the treatment of women through the tale.

The Monk's clothing makes him one of the most complex characters when analyzing this form of symbolism. With the other pilgrims, it is clear what type of morals they have, as well as their class. However, the Monk does not fall on either side. Monks are meant to be completely devoted to God and swear off earthly goods. Despite this, the Monk in the text is described as wearing fashionable clothing sleeves lined with squirrel fur, well-made boots and a gold pin. When reading this, most assume that he is full of greed and lacks devotion to God. However, on further inspection the monk is more complicated. In the article A Reconsideration of the Monk's Clothing, Laura Hodges explains the Monk's clothing by stating, "an examination of costume details in historical context places it within a range of ordinary array worn by a late fourteenth-century monk of his degree in spite of the fact that it does not conform completely to the Benedictine Rule and subsequent sumptuary ordinances" (Hodges 2). Chaucer depicts an accurate example of monk through his character white also satirizing the class itself. Monks presented themselves above the material world, and through his character, Chaucer reveals the truth of most monks' behavior, proving them to be hypocritical and wanting just like everyone else.

Through the description of these character's choice of dress, the reader can understand how Chaucer uses symbolism to satirize the social classes, especially with the members of the clergy. He often depicts them as greedy and materialistic by describing them being dressed in expensive and fashionable clothing. This form of symbolism also hinted at the personalities and morals of the pilgrims themselves, which undoubtedly affected their writing. The clothing also sets the time of the tales, as clothing can often be traced back to specific time periods.

Other examples of symbolism can be shown through the characters' physiognomy in both the General Prologue and in the tales. Physiognomy is the study of analyzing a person, or in this case character's personality, beliefs, and morals based on their outward appearance, mainly regarding their face. This is specifically shown in Chaucer's The Canterbury Tales. through physiognomy in the General Prologue and in the pilgrim's tales. The characters that best represent the physiognomic symbolism in the General Prologue are the Merchant, the Squire, and Pardoner.

The Merchant was described as worthy and dignified. However, his physiognomy of the character says otherwise. This is specifically shown through his facial hair. His forked beard shows the duality between his appearance and his profession. He resembles a businessman who is both successful and reliable. But, following the theme of the tales, things aren't always as they appear under the surface. The text states, "This worthy man employed his wit very well: There was no one who knew that he was in debt..." (Chaucer

279-280). The Merchant was struggling with financial security and lying to his customers by telling them he was selling them "Religious relics." The merchant appeared one way, however, his physiognomy revealed that his character was actually very different than it seemed at first glance.

The physiognomy of the Squire shows his character as youthful and chivalric. This aspect of his character also further backs up the symbolism shown through his clothing previously discussed. The Squire is described in the text as, "a lover and a lively bachelor, with locks curled as if they had been laid in a curler" (Chaucer 80-81). He was handsome, youthful and agile. While this description represents his character, it can be misleading. While many believe this description portrays the Squire as frivolous and disinterested in hard work. However, while he was young and exuberant, he was also prepared to serve the knight thoroughly and work hard to achieve his goals.

The Pardoner is a unique character as the symbolism shown through physiognomy is not immediately apparent as it is with the other characters. The Pardoner is described as having soft blonde hair, glaring eyes, and sharp features. The text states, "This Pardoner had hair as yellow as wax...He had glaring eyes such as has a hare... He had no beard, nor never would have; It (his face) was as smooth as if it were recently shaven" (Chaucer 675-690). These, as well as their other features, are often seen as incredibly feminine. Something that is often not Analyzed by critics. However, Douglas Wurtele analyzed these critiques in his article and explained, "These, by close analogy with both animals and human beings, suggest a variety of pejorative traits. The worst of these are dishonesty and deceitfulness. To be sure, the same physical signs can also suggest hermaphroditism and possibly sodomy" (Wurtele 11). This is supported by the text when Chaucer describes the Pardoner and states, "I believe he was a eunuch or a homosexual" (Chaucer 691). These different possibilities refer to the complexity of the character of the Pardoner and the different interpretations that can be found through the symbolism of his physiognomy.

This connection can be seen when further analyzing physiognomy of characters throughout the Pilgrim' stories. This gives insight into the personality of pilgrims telling the stories, as well as often symbolizing the main themes portrayed through the stories. The clearest examples of this are found in the Tale of Sir Thopas and the Wife of Bath's Tale.

The Tale of Sir Thopas is told by the narrator, who claims to have no skill in storytelling and chooses instead to repeat a story he once heard. In this tale, the narrator describes the main character, a knight called Sir Topaz, as fair and gentle. The text states, "Sir Thopas grew up to be a daughty lad; white was his face as fine white bread, his lips red as rose; his complexion is like scarlet deeply dyed..." (Chaucer 724-727). His boyish and unblemished complexion symbolizes the difference between Sir Topaz and what is considered a normal knight. During this time, knights were hard workers and battle-worn. They were not materialistic or boastful, and they often had scars or other blemishes on their face due to their manual labor and battles. However, Sir Thopas didn't carry any of these marks that would portray him as a stereotypical knight. In fact, he looked similar to how a prince or a noble would.

A second good example of the use of physiognomy in the pilgrim's tales is in the Wife of Bath's Tale. The appearance of the old woman is in direct contrast with the truth, which only further backs up the theme of the tale. The old woman is described in the text as, "so loathsome, and so old..." (Chaucer 1100). Despite this description of the old woman being ugly, she is revealed to be a beautiful young woman who has concealed the truth using magic. This shows that while Chaucer uses physiognomy to reveal who a character truly is, he also uses it to hide the truth in order to further the plot.

Physiognomy is the study of analyzing a person's nature based on their appearance, especially their facial features. It deepens the characters' personalities and their morals. These examples not only clearly display the connection between the symbolism shown in both the Pilgrims and the characters in their stories, but also furthers the points Chaucer was making on the flaws of the different social classes throughout the entire text.

Character representation is an important form of symbolism in The Canterbury Tales. During the time the text was written, Chaucer was immensely critical of the different social classes. He categorized his characters into three main groups, nobility, clergy, and peasants. This is further explained by D.S. Brewer in their article Class Distinction in Chaucer. Brewer states, "The functional system thus treats all persons as potentially equal in one sense, wherever their actual occupation...It is therefore an essential part of Chaucer's social satire in the General Prologue." (Brewer 15). Chaucer used the equality the pilgrims had through their journey to point out the flaws of the different characters. By doing this, as well as through the descriptions of the characters, Chaucer was able to satirize these three main social classes through the distinct groups of pilgrims, as well as prevent backlash for his harsh critiques as he was technically critiquing the characters, not society directly.

The clearest example of nobility in The Canterbury Tales is the Knight. Chaucer did this for two main reasons, the first reason being that it would not make sense to have nobility travelling with both the clergy and the working class. The nobility, when going on a pilgrimage, would usually travel in their own group with guards. The second reason Chaucer did this was because he did not want to receive any repercussions for directly critiquing the nobility.

Brewer analyzes this character, stating, "This is the description of the Knight in the General Prologue, where the moral beauty of the ideal is so finely portrayed in a personal and class portrait whose power endures today..." (Brewer 12). Chaucer used the Knight's character to portray how a knight, and subsequently how a noble, should behave. The Knight was honorable and brave, as was traditional for that character, unlike how Chaucer portrayed many of his other characters, often pointing out their flaws in order to critique the classes they represent.

The second group, the clergy, is made-up of the Prioress, the two nuns, the Monk, the Friar, the Parson, and the Pardoner. The Parson is described as different from the rest of the characters of the clergy. The General Prologue states, "he was rich in holy thought and work. He was also a learned man, a scholar, Who would preach Christ's gospel truly; He would devoutly teach his parishioners. He was gracious, and wonderfully diligent, And very patient in a dversity..." (Chaucer 480-484). He was kind and honorable, everything that the members of the clergy proclaimed themselves to be. With the exception of the Parson, the rest of these characters were heavily critiqued by Chaucer as being hypocritical and full of greed for earthly goods. Chaucer uses these contrasting characters to symbolize the clergy and their actions during that time. The Parson represents what the clergy should be, honest and just, while the other characters represent what the clergy truly was, dishonest and corrupt.

The third and final group is the working class. This group is c omposed of any character who didn't fall into the nobility or clergy classes. The duality of these characters tends to contradict itself, while also adding to the theme of complexity with these characters. Chaucer portrays some of the working class in a negative way. Such as, the Merchant, the Reeve, and the Miller. He depicts them as dishonest and somewhat immoral. Brewer explains, "The fraudulent Manciple, the unwholesome "harlot" the Summoner, the hypocritical swindling Pardoner...But one needs to make sure when the usage is serious, and when ironic" (Brewer 12). Chaucer used description to both critique the social classes and to add humor to the text.

However, with other characters, for example, the Cook and the Plowman. He presents these two characters in a more positive light. He shows them to be honest, hardworking, and taking pride in what they do. Chaucer does this to acknowledge both the flaws and the strengths found within the characters of the working class, and how these people are neither good nor bad.

While Chaucer is critiquing the different social classes of society during that time, he is also providing insight into what it was like during that time from the point of views of the different social classes, and how that could either improve or corrupt a person's character.

Throughout The Canterbury Tales, Chaucer often uses symbolism to further the identity of the characters and provide satirical critiques on society during that time, especially with the classes of the nobility and clergy. Chaucer also uses symbolism through setting to not only provide an accurate story based on the time and place of where the story is set, but also introduce themes that will be uncovered throughout the story through the symbolism. Chaucer uses physiognomy and clothing to further the characters' identities as well as to portray how they act, their place in society during that time, and gives a good idea of their social classes when he is critiquing them.

Bibliography

Brewer, D. S. "Class Distinction in Chaucer." Speculum, vol. 43, no. 2, 1968, pp. 290–305. JSTOR, https://doi.org/10.2307/2855936. Accessed 23 Apr. 2024.

Chaucer, Geoffrey. "The Canterbury Tales". Harvard University, https://chaucer.fas.harvard.edu/pages/text-and-translations. Accessed 23 Apr. 2024.

Hodges, Laura F. "A Reconsideration of the Monk's Costume." The Chaucer Review, vol. 26, no. 2, 1991, pp. 133–46. JSTOR, http://www.jstor.org/stable/25094190. Accessed 23 Apr. 2024.

Wurtele, Douglas. "Some Uses of Physiognomical Lore in Chaucer's 'Canterbury Tales.'" The Chaucer Review, vol. 17, no. 2, 1982, pp. 130–41. JSTOR, http://www.jstor.org/stable/25093823. Accessed 23 Apr. 2024.

Chivalry in Sir Gawain and the Green Knight
Savanna Peveto-Kreatschman

Sir Gawin is a 14th century chivalric romance written by an anonymous author known as the Gawain Poet, or The Pearl Poet. It was written in Middle English alliterative verse. In fact, it is one of the four major poems that make up the Alliterative Revival, a movement in Middle English in which long tales or poems were told using ample alliteration. Sir Gwain and the Green Knight, written by the Gawain Poet, explores the themes of chivalry and honor, as is common in classical Arthurian legends. The main ways these themes were shown were Sir Gawain accepting the challenge, honoring his hosts, and fulfilling his promises; even when breaking his host's trusts, he did what he could to repent and not make those mistakes again.

The story focuses on Sir Gawain, a knight of King Arthur's Court. Sir Gawain is not only Arthur's knight, but also his nephew, making him one of Arthur's knights. This is shown in the beginning of the tale by Sir Gawain's seat at the table, which as the tale states, "There good Gawain was seated beside Guinevere." As the Queen was seen as a particularly important figure and inspiration to many Knights, it was an honor for someone to be able to sit next to her at the table. During a celebration at King Arthur's court, a mysterious and dangerous Green Knight comes to Arthur's court. Greg Walker, writer of the article "Courtesy and Chivalry in *Sir Gawain and the Green Knight*" in the Cambridge Press, explains "The Green Knight in himself represents an unsettling mixture of the monstrous and the decorous, the chivalrous and civilised and their barbarous, incomprehensible, opposites." The Knight, by being opposite in character, highlights Sir Gawain's virtues. The Green Knight challenges the Knights of the Round Table to a deadly game: someone would strike the Green Knight with his own axe, and in one year and one day he would come and return the favor. When no one stepped forward, the king prepared to take on the challenge, but Sir Gawin, understanding the Knight's role and duty to his king, took the place of King Arthur.

The tale is a notable example of the Chivalric Code knights followed in the 6th century, the time Arthurian tales such as this were set in. This code provides a list of virtues each knight should possess. The story gives these attributes through, as Walker explains, "exchanges between Arthur, Gawain and the Knight, in which the nature of a crucial nexus of elite values: kingship, heroism, chivalric honour and courtliness, are subjected to a subtle but determined scrutiny and re-evaluation." A knight found lacking in these virtues was considered dishonorable and a disgrace to knighthood. Throughout the tale, Sir Gawain represents these virtues and the importance of following the code, as well as what consequences could come from breaking it.

Sir Gawain accepted the challenge out of duty to his king. During this time, it was a knight's job to put himself second and protect his king or his Lord at any cost. When no knight stepped forward, the King decided to take on the challenge to preserve the pride of his court. Not allowing the king to take on such a dangerous game, which could be fatal, Sir Gawain stepped forward to take his place. He decapitated the Green Knight, who then picked up his head and announced that Sir Gawain should come to him at the Green Chapel in one year to finish the challenge. Being an honorable knight, after one year and one day, he prepared to journey to the Green Chapel. In the tale, Gawin explains to the courtiers of Arthur's court, "'What should I fear?' he said; For whether kind or harsh A man's fate must be tried.'" This is an example of Sir Gawain's bravery and commitment, as, despite knowing that he might not return from this fatal journey, and many of those who knew him had already started to mourn him, he honored his promise and took on the responsibilities of his commitment.

Sir Gawain struggled to follow the chivalric code as his host's wife attempted to draw him into a situation where he would have no choice but to go against the code in some way. During his travels, Sir Gawain came to a clearing. It was here that he stopped and prayed until a castle appeared. He was warmly welcomed by the Lord, Bertilak de Hautdesert. However, while he stayed there, the wife of Bertilak continuously made passes at him. At first, he was able to deny her, but soon the lady started to pressure him into returning her flirtations. Sir Gawain was then, according to Walker, "faced with a choice between adultery and discourtesy." He was forced to choose between going against his host's kindness or offending the lady's pride, both of which broke the code of chivalry.

As time went on, Sir Gawain slowly started falling into the temptation to break the code of chivalry by hiding information that his host requested. During this same time, the host had convinced Sir Gawain to play a game: Sir Gawain would spend three days relaxing with the ladies at the castle, while at the same time, Lord Bertilak would go hunting. At the end of each day, they would get together and exchange what they had gained. For the first two nights, all went according to the rules of the game; Lord Bertilak had exchanged the animals he had caught, while Sir Gawain had given kisses to the Lord, equal to the amount that the Lady had given him. However, Sir Gawain had not revealed to the Lord who had given him the kisses. When the lord asked, Gawain's reply was, "'That was not in our agreement' said he, 'ask nothing else; For you have had what is due to you, expect to receive nothing more.'" While this was not technically deceitful, he was not being completely honest with his generous host.

On the third day, Sir Gawain made a selfish decision, and in this, broke the chivalric code. Along with three kisses, Sir Gawain was also gifted a girdle that would protect him from any mortal injury. Wanting to protect himself from the Green Knight, he accepted the girdle. When it came time for the exchange that night, Sir Gawain gave his host three kisses, but abstained from revealing the girdle, instead keeping it for himself. This was the true violation of the code of chivalry. Not only did he deceive his gracious host, but he also planned to use the girdle to cheat in the challenge with the Green Knight. Sir Gawain, knowing his dishonesty, went to confession in the church, and as the tale explains, "There he confessed himself honestly and admitted his sins, Both the great and the small, and forgiveness begs, and calls on the priest for absolution." However, he still decided to keep the girdle despite knowing the dishonor in his actions. Up to this point, Sir Gawain had been the perfect representation of chivalric ideals.

Sir Gawain displayed courage through his determination to finish the journey and complete the challenge. After his six days' rest at Lord Bertilak's castle, Sir Gawain set off to confront the Green Knight. Despite his fear, which was only worsened by others telling him that he would not survive, and he would not be judged if he chose not to go through with it, he did not back down. He explained to a servant who was attempting to convince him to abandon his quest, "'if I avoided this place, Took to my heels in fright, in the way you propose, I should be a cowardly knight, and could not be excused.'" This is a prime example of his courage, honor and commitment, all key points of the chivalric code.

When discovering the Green Knight's identity, Sir Gawain was shown the importance of chivalry through all factors of life. Once he arrived at the Green Chapel, he was greeted by the Green Knight, who once again reiterated the rules. Sir Gawain got in position and prepared himself for the blow. The Green Knight then feigned blows twice, before swinging his axe and delivering only a small knick against Gawain's neck. It was then revealed that the Green Knight was Lord Bertilak, who sent his wife to flirt with Sir Gawain to test his honor. The first two feigned blows represented the first two nights in which Sir Gwain had honored their deal. However, the knick was the consequence for hiding the girdle from his host, therefore breaking the agreed upon rules and the host's trust.

After revealing his identity, Lord Bertilak states, "'True men must pay back truly, Then he need nothing fear; You failed me the third time And took that blow therefore.'" Through the challenge, the Green Knight had impressed upon Sir Gawain the importance of following the chivalric code, for if he had, he would have completed the challenge completely unharmed.

As a way to repent for his mistake and as a reminder of what he had done, Sir Gwain decided to keep the girdle, saying, "'For the cowardice and covetousness that seized me there; This is the token of the dishonesty I was caught committing, And now I must wear it as long as I live.'" The girdle is symbolic of the vices and temptations that a knight could easily fall prey to but must guard against as they follow the chivalric code. King Arthur's court, out of respect and loyalty to Sir Gawain, followed his lead by adopting a green sash into their wardrobe. These sashes stood as symbols of chivalry and knighthood, and all the virtues that accompanied them, as well as the shame that came from dishonorable actions.

Sir Gawain and the Green Knight is a chivalric romance that highlights the many virtues of a good knight. It does this by emphasizing Sir Gawain's honorable actions and the ways he tries to repent and reconcile his mistakes. Throughout the tale, many important themes are explored. Such as, the importance of being honest and acting honorably no matter the situation.

Bibliography

Translated by James Winny. "Sir Gawain and the Green Knight." Broadwayview Press, 1995.

Walker G. Courtesy and Chivalry in Sir Gawain and the Green Knight. In: Reading Literature Historically: Drama and Poetry from Chaucer to the Reformation. Edinburgh University Press; 2013:93-120.

Art

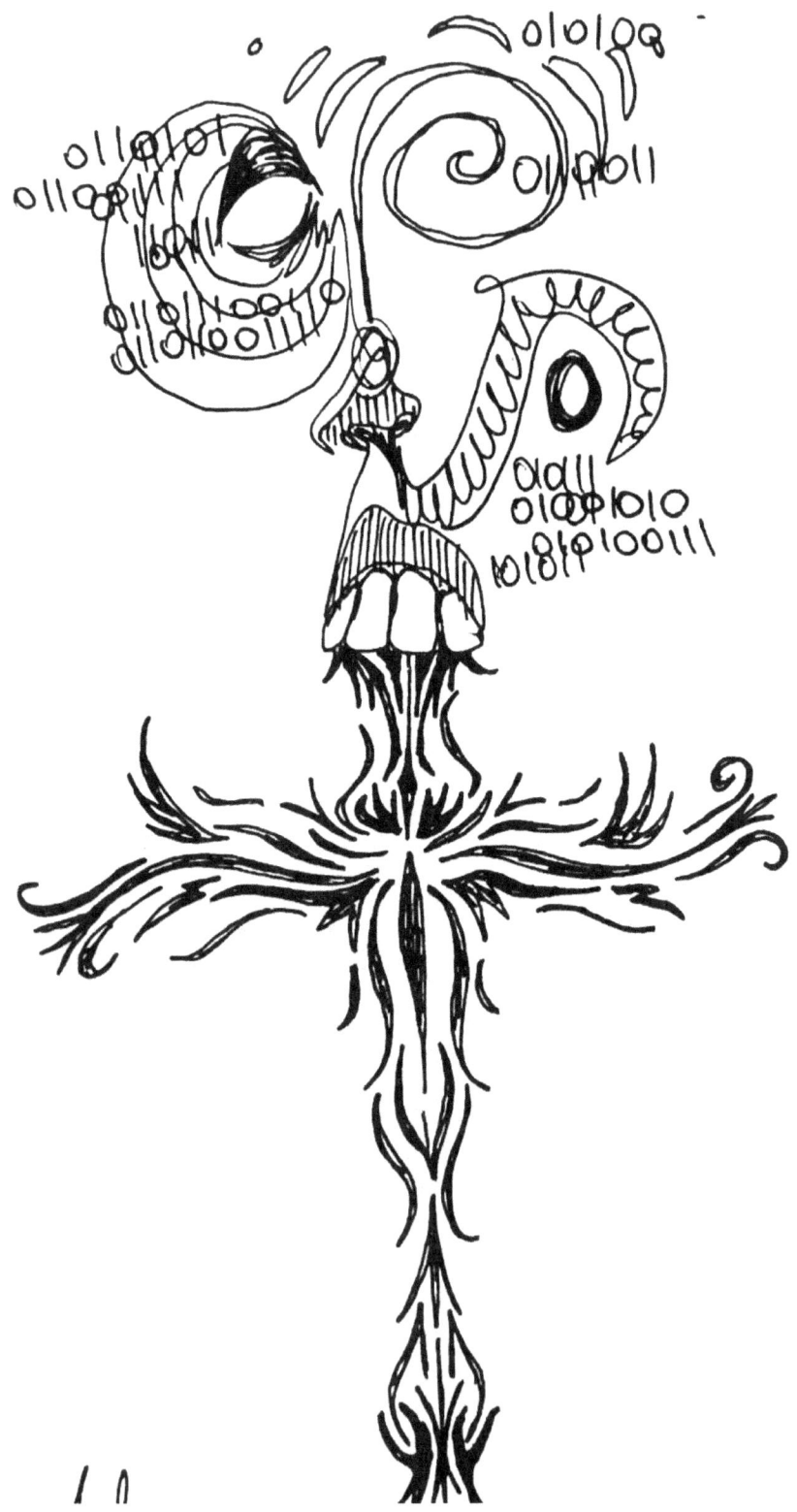

Contributor Biographies

Mikaela Bartlett
Mikaela Bartlett is an English major with a minor in Communications. She's currently working in the English Department as the typesetter for Pulse! Some of her other hobbies include reading, baking, music, theater, and playing with her dogs, Zola and Rafael. Mikaela has been writing all kinds of things for as long as she can remember, but poetry has always held a special place in her heart. She's grateful for this opportunity to share her poems and be a part of Pulse!

Mae Bradley
Mae Bradley is a senior pursuing a Bachelor's in English, minoring in philosophy, writing, and Spanish. She uses her multilingual skillset to assert a flexibility of vocabulary that makes her poetry uniquely expressive. She writes for herself alone, creating deeply emotional pieces, each with their own voice and personality meant to display each facet of her character.

Erica Callahan
Erica Callahan is a sophomore Civil Engineering. She has a passion for all things arts and science. Her poetry is often inspired by the small and overlooked moments in life. She hopes to capture the weird feeling of being alive.

Aaron Cloud
Aaron Cloud, from Nederland, Texas, is a junior majoring in History at Lamar University with a minor in Writing. In a creative writing course taken in the fall of 2024, Aaron wrote "The Entity," a short story inspired by Lovecraftian horror, for peer review. After a handful of revisions, the story was submitted to Pulse.

Claudia Cooper
This is Claudia's third year as Pulse prose editor, first year as co-editor-in-chief, and second time contributing to Pulse. She enjoys all things creative, whether singing, writing, dancing, or making visual art. Please don't make her do math and logic.

Vanessa Davis
Vanessa Davis is currently a junior at Lamar University and is pursuing a bachelor's degree in English and History. Vanessa thoroughly enjoys activities such as baton twirling, reading,

visiting museums, and going on random little adventures. After Vanessa obtains her degree, she plans to go into a law enforcement or wildlife conservation field, with her dream career being Game Warden.

Megan Docter
Megan is a figurative artist whose work encompasses both traditional and digital mediums, including charcoal, pen and ink, and Clip Studio Paint. Over the last few months she has begun experimenting with various painting styles, taking inspiration from artists like Darrell Troppy and Lucian Freud, and exploring various painting mediums and supports including oil, water soluble oil, wax, cardboard, and paper.

Kowen Ducote
Kowen Ducote is a physics student at Lamar University with a passion for writing and inspiring change in others. He speaks on a variety of social issues in his writing, with a particular commitment to dismantling violent ideals. When Kowen isn't taking his ideas to paper, he can be found studying, boxing, playing music, or spending time with friends.

Shelby Eason
Shelby Eason is a current actor in Lamar University's Theatre & Dance program with plans to graduate in December of 2025. When she isn't working in main stage productions, she's busy writing poetry and short stories that she hopes inspire others to share their inner artist, no matter how small.

Crystal Figueroa
Currently a senior at Lamar University, Crystal finds joy in the pages of poetry and romance novels. Beyond her studies, she shares her lifelong passion for dance by teaching professional and competitive techniques at the studio where her journey began at the age of two. Known for her sensitivity, Crystal discovers profound meaning in the small intricacies of life, an emotional connection that frequently inspires her to write poetry.

Yoseli González
Yoseli González Rodríguez is a 19 year old actress, artist, and starting writer from Puerto Rico. With acting as her main passion, Yoseli has worked in theatrical productions, films, and commercials. But a love for classic literature has inspired many drawings and pieces of writing she hopes to continue publishing. Currently,

Yoseli is highly involved in Lamar University's Theater and Dance Department and film crews with digital art commissions on the side as well as a couple of passion projects that she will continue to craft.

Nyah Greene
Nyah Greene is a Bahamian American studying as a Fine Arts student with a concentration in drawing. She plans on taking the techniques she's learned over the years at Lamar University and becoming a tattoo artist running her tattoo studio as well as working in a museum upon graduating.

Grace Harmon
Allison Grace Harmon (P.M.) is an English major working as a graduate assistant within Lamar University's English Department. She does in fact enjoy pina coladas and getting caught in the rain. In her free time, she enjoys playing Skyrim and avoiding her deadlines.

Paxton Holmes
Paxton Holmes, a nineteen year-old from Beaumont, Texas. She was born and raised in Beaumont, Texas and is currently a freshman at Lamar University. She is an English major with a focus in teaching and minoring in Art History. She plans on going on to teach after graduating.

Mohamed Irhabi
Mohamed Irhabi is a Pre-Med scholar at Lamar University and recipient of the prestigious David J. Beck Fellowship. He actively engages in research and community service, regularly attends & presents at conferences, and finds inspiration in creative writing, volunteerism, and martial arts.

Jiyoon Jeon
Jiyoon Jeon, a prospective neuroscientist-physician from South Korea, blends her expertise in science and passion for social justice. With degrees in biotechnology, forensic science, and molecular biology, her work explores the intersection of trauma, medicine, and humanities. A lover of languages and creativity, she expresses herself through multilingual poetry.

Gaberielle LaRocca
Gaberielle LaRocca is a first-generation Social Work student set to graduate in May 2025. She is actively involved in several

organizations, including Alpha Omega Epsilon, the Social Work Student Association, Order of Omega, and Omicron Delta Kappa. Currently she is interning at Spindletop Center, and the M.I.N.D Project on campus.

Britton Larson
Britton Larson is a poetry reader for this publication. This is his 3rd year on the Pulse staff. He graduated in Fall 2024 with his Bachelor's degree in English and hopes to continue his education in grad school. If he can't make that happen, this is probably the last you will see of him. If he can, expect to see him here again.

Chloe Lopez
Chloe Lopez is a senior English student at Lamar University. Her written works handle topics such as horror, the Gothic, and how the two manifest in the modern world, religion, and the American South. Chloe's interests include Southern Gothic, writing her debut novel, horror media, artists like Ethel Cain, and generally foreboding forests.

Lupe Lopez
Lupe Lopez is a Southeast Texas artist, well rounded in many traditional and digital mediums. With a knack for creating and offering creative thoughts to fellow peers. Hoping to one day become an illustrator for children's books or storyboard artist.

Cheyenne Lunsford
As a twenty-one-year-old junior in college, Cheyenne has always found a voice in her writing. She loves using her poetry to find beauty in the ashes. As she is studying English and American Sign Language, Cheyenne aspires to give a voice to those who have none. Whether it be children or adults, her passion is showing the world that they too can be seen.

Davonna Martin
DaVonna Martin is a senior at Lamar University studying American Sign Language. She found her love of writing poetry due to her sister writing as well, and with the need to express herself through her poems!

Kayla McKinley
Kayla McKinley is a Pre-Physical Therapy Exercise Science major. This year will be her second time contributing for Pulse. Outside of class, she enjoys being involved in various student organizations,

contributing for Cadenza and conducting undergraduate research at Lamar University. She is very honored to share an essay on food insecurity for publication in Pulse!

Erin Medley
Erin Medley is a studio arts major with a concentration in drawing and will be expected to graduate in the Fall of 2025. She works primarily in charcoal and chalk pastel. Outside of art, she enjoys listening to music and learning to play guitar.

Aubreigh Moses
Aubreigh is a studio drawing major who expresses her thoughts and ideas through her artwork. Her work focuses on religious symbolism and explores personal identity. When she isn't sketching, she enjoys writing music and spending time with her friends. In the future, she plans to learn animation so she can bring her drawings to life.

Savanna Peveto-Kreatschman
Savanna Peveto-Kreatschman is a senior who is majoring in English and minoring in writing. She loves reading, writing short stories, crocheting, and spending time with friends and family. In the future she hopes to earn a masters in English and doctorate in Library Science, and work university level as a librarian and English professor.

Jarely Rebollar
Jarely Rebollar is a first-generation Mexican American writer from Beaumont, Texas. She graduated from Lamar University with a bachelor's degree in Psychology and a minor in Writing. Passionate about education, storytelling, and cultural identity, she explores themes of resilience and heritage in her work. She hopes to inspire others through her writing and advocacy.

Moya Rose
Moya Rose is a poet and novelist whose work cracks open the world to examine its fractures and fleeting light. Her poems—unflinching yet lyrical—grapple with race, love, and the weight of social injustice, stitching personal ache into collective reckoning. When she isn't writing poems that simmer with defiance and tenderness, she's crafting novels that pulse with the same urgency. A devourer of stories and a wielder of words, she believes language can both wound and mend. This is her first published poem, a beginning.

Erika Valiente
Erika Valiente is a pre-nursing student at Lamar University who writes for self-expression. After years of facing a culture identity crisis, she shares her story as a Mexican American daughter and the challenges that come with a language barrier. With her personal narrative, she hopes to represent second-generation individuals who struggle to be heard.

Gabriela Valiente
Gabriela Valiente earned her Bachelor's Degree in Graphic Design from Lamar University. As she adjusts to post-grad life, she reads and writes to keep her mind active. She hopes to one day write a screenplay or publish a book.

Keely Viator
Keely Viator is a graduate English major with a particular interest in both creative prose and poetry. She loves discussing character creation and development for use in written works, as it lets her explore new perspectives. After graduating, she hopes to continue building on her style and desire for creative expression.

Rylee Wenzel
Rylee Wenzel is a senior at Lamar University and will be graduating in May of 2025. She is pursuing a bachelor's degree in English with a minor in Writing. This summer, she will be furthering her education as a graduate student. She aspires to work in the publishing industry.

Kensi MacCammond Williams
Kensi MacCammond Williams is an English graduate student at Lamar University where she has been able to greatly further her knowledge and love for reading and writing. Her top interests include, but are not limited to, any and all horror books/movies she can get her hands on and blasting lots of great rock'n'roll tunes.

Teri Wolfe
Teri Wolfe is in the process of getting her master's degree in English at Lamar University. She has an interest in the arts—particularly writing, drawing, music, and theatre. While she likes to create her own works, she finds enjoyment in other people's creations and gets easily inspired from their contagious passion to create. With her degree, she plans on becoming an instructor, or a comic book illustrator and writer (whichever comes first).

Danny Young

Danny Young is an undergraduate student at Lamar University who specializes in fiction writing. They were born and raised in southeast Texas and enjoy writing stories set in the south. Most of their inspiration is taken from their upbringing, and the experiences of others within their community.

Pulse Staff Biographies

Keely Viator, Editor in Chief
Keely Viator is a graduate English major with a particular interest in both creative prose and poetry. She loves discussing character creation and development for use in written works, as it lets her explore new perspectives. After graduating, she hopes to continue building on her style and desire for creative expression.

Claudia Cooper, Editor in Chief, Prose Editor
This is Claudia's third year as Pulse prose editor, first year as co-editor-in-chief, and second time contributing to Pulse. She enjoys all things creative, whether singing, writing, dancing, or making visual art. Please don't make her do math and logic.

Mikaela Bartlett, Typesetter, Poetry Reader
Mikaela Bartlett is an English major with a minor in Communications. She's currently working in the English Department as the typesetter for Pulse! Some of her other hobbies include reading, baking, music, theater, and playing with her dogs, Zola and Rafael. Mikaela has been writing all kinds of things for as long as she can remember, but poetry has always held a special place in her heart. She's grateful for this opportunity to share her poems and be a part of Pulse!

Britton Larson, Poetry Editor
Britton Larson is a poetry reader for this publication. This is his 3rd year on the Pulse staff. He graduated in Fall 2024 with his Bachelor's degree in English and hopes to continue his education in grad school. If he can't make that happen, this is probably the last you will see of him. If he can, expect to see him here again.

Mae Bradley, Poetry Editor
Mae Bradley is a senior pursuing a Bachelor's in English, minoring in philosophy, writing, and Spanish. She uses her multilingual skillset to assert a flexibility of vocabulary that makes her poetry uniquely expressive. She writes for herself alone, creating deeply emotional pieces, each with their own voice and personality meant to display each facet of her character.

Savanna Peveto-Kreatschman, Prose Editor
Savanna Peveto-Kreatschman is a senior who is majoring in English and minoring in writing. She loves reading, writing short

stories, crocheting, and spending time with friends and family. In the future she hopes to earn a masters in English and doctorate in Library Science, and work university level as a librarian and English professor.

Erica Callahan, Poetry Reader
Erica Callahan is a sophomore Civil Engineering. She has a passion for all things arts and science. Her poetry is often inspired by the small and overlooked moments in life. She hopes to capture the weird feeling of being alive.

Isabella Deese, Poetry Reader
Isabella Deese is a reader for Pulse Magazine and a member of the English Honor society, Sigma Tua Delta. Isabella was published in Pulse in 2023 with her single poem "Today", which is unofficially dedicated to Michele Brown who passed a month before the 2022-2023 edition was released.

Grace Nicholson, Prose Reader
Grace Nicholson A.M., Graduate of English in the Department of English and Modern Languages, likes to live life on the safe side. If you encounter this creature, know that she is in need of a London Fog, a warm blanket, and a sound machine that makes thunderstorm noises. Talk books with her. Be kind.

Grace Harmon, Prose Reader
Allison Grace Harmon (P.M.) is an English major working as a graduate assistant within Lamar University's English Department. She does in fact enjoy pina coladas and getting caught in the rain. In her free time, she enjoys playing Skyrim and avoiding her deadlines.

Jazmin Gonzalez, Prose Reader
Jazmin Gonzalez has always had a passion for writing and poetry. She is currently a graduate student aiming to receive her master's degree in English, while working full-time as a high school teacher.